# Deadly Desire

Kate Allenton

Discover other titles by Kate Allenton

At


<u>www.kateallenton.com</u>



Cover Image Created by:
**<u>http://www.two26media.com</u>**

# DEDICATION

Dedicated to Sara Dowd

For whom my character was named after.

Congratulations on your upcoming nuptials.

May you and Nathan find your

happily ever after.

# ACKNOWLEDGMENTS

A Special Thanks goes to Sandy Link for her
top notch editing.

And Ilse for being my last line of defense and
my trusted beta reader.

And also

Joshua Samolewicz for amazing work on my book
covers, even when I'm being difficult and picky.

# 1 CHAPTER

Ex-FBI Agent Sara Johnson rushed through the halls of her new office building in downtown Kodiak Falls and pushed through the freshly painted conference room door, trying to catch her breath.

"Sorry," she mumbled to the assembled group. She was late again but, this time, it wasn't really her fault. When her father got on a rampage, it was hard to get him off the phone, and he was definitely on another rampage.

Her chest tightened as she remembered their latest conversation and how she'd tried to laugh off the hurt. Spouting the words "disinherit" and "disown" was becoming second nature to the assistant deputy director of the FBI. It seemed she could do nothing right in his eyes, another embarrassment she didn't know how to fix. Her latest mistake had been making the headlines in the gossip rags. She sighed and slipped into a seat between her two best friends and braced herself for the teasing to begin; and, it would be coming. She dropped the manila envelope on the table and waited. One…two…

Sara didn't even make it to three before Lexi Hathaway, her newly engaged best friend, leaned into her. "Loved the knee-high socks. They really helped rock the plaid schoolgirl mini skirt."

Sara was helpless against stopping the heat from creeping into her cheeks.

Catherine leaned in from the other side. "They went perfectly with the tied-up white shirt and pigtails."

Sara cupped her face and shook her head because a quick and witty retort eluded her.

Garrett chuckled from across the table. "I must admit the spy glasses were not only useful but a perfect complement to the outfit."

Sara groaned as she lifted her face and pegged her coworker with a glare. "The reporters weren't even supposed to know I was there." She tilted her head. "You wouldn't know anything about that…would you?"

Garrett's teasing grin turned into a deep-rooted frown. "You know I would never do anything to hurt you. I was just teasing."

Marco Hill, Lexi's business partner and co-owner of Carrington-Hill Investigations, stood at the end of the long cherry table clutching a copy of the morning paper. His usually expressionless face wasn't so expressionless today as he cleared his throat and gave Sara a hard disapproving smile.

"It seems Ms. Johnson has done it again."

Immediately the song of the pop star she had dressed to imitate started playing in her head. *Damn it.* He tossed the paper into the middle of the table as Sara tucked a stray strand of hair behind her ear. She reminded herself that dressing for undercover work was just part of the job, something she couldn't get around. *Suck it up, Johnson.* "I can explain?"

He gave her a pointed look that seemed to indicate she'd never come up with an explanation that could counteract the proof of the picture. "Sara, is the word *discretion* even in your vocabulary?"

Would this nightmare ever end? Bad enough she'd been busted leaving the underground club, but now the proof sat in living color in front of her for all of the world to see. Okay, maybe not all of the world, but enough of it to ensure she'd be teased and taunted for a long while to come.

Lexi and Catherine chuckled before Lexi spoke on her behalf. "Give her a break, Marco. She was just doing her job, and she got the pictures you wanted."

Lexi leaned into her and whispered, "You did get the pictures, right?"

Sara nodded with confidence and pushed the manila folder down the table. "Senator Boyles has been a very naughty boy." She inclined her head toward the package, knowing how Marco loved pictures as proof. She'd taken the pictures herself. The senator was dressed in leather chaps, shirtless, and holding a whip in his hand, the one he used to hit the half-dressed red-headed woman chained to the bars. They had both been too busy enjoying the play to notice the waitress happily snapping pictures with a tiny camera hidden in her nerdy black-rimmed glasses.

It had taken months to worm her way into the exclusive, very secretive underground club. Her snitches with the FBI had vouched for her to the club owner; they said she could be trusted. As if they themselves were trustworthy. Her cover wasn't as a patron. It was as a waitress at the club, appropriately named The Forbidden Fruit. Her risqué uniform provided no room to hide a weapon anywhere on her body. She'd refrained from retaliating against the clientele with the wandering hands and roaming eyes. The experience had pushed the boundaries of her self-control, but she'd prevailed.

Garrett let out a low whistle. "Nice legs, Johnson."

She glanced at him. "Bite me."

He winked. "Anytime, honey…anytime."

Marco lifted the envelope and pulled a picture out halfway. Unable to suppress his approval, he grinned and pushed the photo back inside. "Good job, Sara." He slid another file across the expanse of the cherry table in her direction. "I've got another assignment for you."

An unfamiliar sense of overwhelming pride infused her.

Garrett grinned and wiggled his eyebrows. "I hope it involves her wearing the same type of clothes." He winked. "I still need a date for Lexi's wedding."

"Give it up, G. I'd rather go stag."

They were truly friends and she knew Garrett was just teasing her. He was good looking enough, but she'd never test the boundaries of their friendship. She liked him too much in the status of friends, where she kept him nice and tucked away.

Catherine snorted and elbowed her. "I hope it's more than a cheating husband."

Her pride in getting the job done was short lived.

Marco's face remained passive as he waited for the light-hearted banter to stop. Gone was the satisfaction she'd witnessed moments ago. His lips pulled into a fine line. "The senator's file contains more than just his exploits. He's into some heavy shit."

She nodded and cleared her throat as she flipped the file open on her latest assignment and froze. An eight-by-ten glossy photo of a man the papers had deemed the "world's most eligible bachelor" stared back at her, and damn, he was fine. Her mouth parted, and she was sure she drooled, just a little, as both of her friends leaned in for a closer look. Sara knew his name without looking. She glanced up at Marco.

"Problem, Ms. Johnson?"

Sara leaned back in her chair and crossed her legs. "Seriously? Collin Martin?"

She glanced back down at the picture and started flipping through the file for some hint that this was a practical joke. "What's his story? Someone finally break his heart and he wants us to find out why?"

Marco leaned back in his chair and steepled his fingers in front of him.

She suppressed a giggle and tilted her head. Unable to hide a smile, she tried for the best serious-business voice she could muster. "Suing a plastic surgeon, or, oh, I know... he's suing his manicurist over a hangnail." She grinned as she nodded. "I'm right, aren't I?"

"Murder," a deep voice said from the doorway behind her.

"In the library with a candlestick." The words flew from her lips before she could stop them. She spun her chair toward the sound of the meeting crasher. Leaning against the wall was the client himself. All six foot two of yummy, drop dead, panty wetting, goodness. Brown disheveled hair, bright blue eyes, high cheekbones kissed by the sun and a body that promised to rock worlds. He gave her a conspiratorial wink and the gates of heaven opened when he grinned. For a brief moment, she thought she heard angels singing above. Even the glint in his eyes contained a sensuous flame that sent her pulse racing. He was shockingly sexy and devastating irresistible. It was no wonder women everywhere had labeled him "god's gift to women" because, unfortunately for her, he was even better looking in person. This man had her libido racing from zero to sixty quicker than a truck full of her favorite Chunky Monkey ice cream dripping with hot fudge, covered with whipped cream and with a cherry on top.

"My ex-girlfriend was killed, in her living room, with a gun, Ms. Johnson."

He stepped into the room. *Just perfect*. She'd embarrassed the client and herself. She felt an inch tall. Murder wasn't something she should joke about. She bit her tongue to school herself against her loose words. "I'm sorry for your loss."

He gave her a slight nod and replaced the smile on his face. The man oozed sex appeal, and she knew instantly that he was going to be a pain in the ass for whoever got stuck on his detail.

Marco's voice pulled her back from her thoughts. "Seems the world's most eligible bachelor is also currently…" He paused for dramatic effect. "…un-dateable."

"Oh good lord, you've got to be kidding me." Sara's hand flew to cover her mouth, but it was already too late. Lexi's and Catherine's eyes widened in disbelief as Sara clenched her eyes closed and lifted her chin to the ceiling. *Am I being punished?* she silently asked.

Collin chuckled as he stepped into the room and slid into a chair at the other end of the table. "Believe it or not, it's true."

She turned back to Marco, effectively dismissing the playboy. "And what's my job? You want me to investigate the murder?"

A mischievous grin played at the corners of Marco's mouth. "Your job is to date him."

Oh, Marco was enjoying this way too much, maybe a little payback. Perhaps for letting the photographer get the drop on her while she was undercover on the Senators case. Marco was out of his freakin' mind. "I'm sorry; did you just say that my assignment is to *date* him?"

"You heard right, Ms. Johnson. It appears some of Mr. Martin's ex-girlfriends are turning up dead and we're going to set you up as the next target."

Lexi nudged her. "Solves your problem for finding a date to my wedding."

# 2 CHAPTER

Sara knowingly entered into some strange situations for the love of her job, but this one topped the cake. And not just any cake, but a slice of the crazy covered in are-you-freaking-out-of-your-mind variety. It wasn't that she had a problem with becoming a target for a killer. No, her problem ran much deeper—dating, in general. She sucked at it. Her palms grew sweaty just thinking about it. She unconsciously shivered. She always managed to screw up her dates by saying inappropriate things at the wrong time or by just being clumsy.

Her stomach became unsettled as she remembered the embarrassment from her last date. What had started out as a great evening turned bad within the first hour of him picking her up. It hadn't taken her long to figure out that the ass was also a lousy and abusive drunk. When he'd walked her to the door and couldn't keep his hands to himself, she'd tried politely, at first, to tell him she wasn't interested. When he'd downright persisted and started groping her, she'd had enough, slugged the jerk, and knocked him flat on his ass. Nope, dating wasn't for her, and she hated first dates, especially with men she didn't know. Especially with men who made her nervous, like Collin Martin. He deserved prim, proper, and beautiful on his arm...everything Sara knew she wasn't.

"Exactly what are you expecting?" she asked in the best back-to-business voice she could muster. No matter how crazy the job sounded, she was still going to try and be professional. She'd save her hysterics for when she didn't have an audience.

"For appearance's sake, you're going to date Mr. Martin in the hopes of catching the killer," Marco replied confidently, as though it would be an easy task.

Sara nervously tapped her foot beneath the table and wiped her palms against her skirt. "What makes Mr. Martin so sure that this has anything to do with him?" She turned to Collin. "No offense, but this could have been a random act of violence." She tilted her head. "I assume the police have already checked out your alibi."

The room fell silent waiting for him to reply, "My alibi is iron clad and has been confirmed." He slid a nondescript brown envelope down the table to her. She peeked inside as he explained. He tilted his head toward the envelope. "I received that in the mail two days ago."

Sara pulled out a typed envelope, addressed to Mr. Martin with no return address.

He gestured to the mail in her hand. "Take a look and tell me what you think."

She pulled out the paper inside. It was a photo copy of a letter made from cut out words and letters from magazines and newspapers that had been glued to the sheet, spelling out a cryptic message. *You belong to me. It's up to you whether they live or die.*

Sara flipped the paper over to examine the back; it was completely blank. She glanced up and waved the paper. "I would hope this is a copy and the original is being handled by forensics."

He nodded. "I'm not a complete idiot, Ms. Johnson."

She shrugged. One right move doesn't make him Einstein either but, really, what did she expect from someone that looked as yummy as him. "I'm sure you have a lot of fans, Mr. Martin. What makes you think that, when we play love birds, the killer will even come after me?"

He gave her a slight nod and held her gaze even as he slid another envelope across the slick table. "This does."

She pulled a newspaper clipping out of an identical envelope and unfolded it. It was a news article about a teacher found murdered in South Carolina. Sara skimmed the article and looked at the grainy black and white picture of the woman. She had long curled hair and a wide smile. She looked as though she could be the girl next door. It didn't appear to be the type of woman she'd expect Collin to date. "I take it this is one of your exes?"

Collin laced his fingers on the tabletop. Sara couldn't help but check out his hands, and not because the old saying implying the sizes of hands and feet matched the size of other anatomy, although that had crossed her mind. If the saying were believed to be true…this man wasn't lacking. No, she'd intended to verify that her suspicions were true; he did indeed get manicures. There wasn't a hangnail in sight; his hands were as smooth as a baby's ass. Oh hell, who was she trying to kid? She was checking to see if the rumors about his potential package were true.

"Ms. Johnson…"

When Collin said her name, Sara tried unsuccessfully to remove the grin from her face so she bit her lip and raised a brow, trying to focus on the problem at hand… and there went her resolve. She groaned, and her gaze flew back to the hands clasped in front of him. Lexi nudged her side, and Sara's gaze flew back up to the client's non-amused face.

"Please continue."

"Mary was my high school sweetheart." He pointed to the clipping. "She was killed right after our fifteen-year reunion, a reunion that I attended."

"And where were you…" She glanced back down at the article. "…on October 31$^{st}$?"

The corners of Collin's lips dipped into a frown. He ran his hand over the sexy stubble on his chin; and, yes, even that was just as sexy as the rest of him. "I was at a Halloween party with two hundred guests."

"That shouldn't be hard to corroborate," Lexi muttered. She again nudged Sara's elbow, reminding her that she was still in the meeting and her bosses were witnesses to the one-on-one conversation she was having with the bachelor. She just hoped she'd masked the overwhelming effect he was having on her. Sara squirmed in her seat.

Marco leaned forward, propping his elbows on the table. "I can vouch for Collin. I was at the same party."

Sara slowly turned her head to Marco. She wasn't sure what shocked her more, the fact that Marco personally knew Collin or imagining him doing anything remotely fun like attending a party. "Really? I can't imagine you at a party, much less a Halloween party, but I'd love to see the pictures."

Marco tapped the table. "This isn't about me, Sara. Let's stay focused." He rose from the table. "You have everything you need to know in that file. Let's regroup in the morning and come up with a plan."

Everyone stood and sauntered out of the room, talking in easy banter. Collin followed Sara into her office. "It was a pleasure to meet you, Ms. Johnson. I'm looking forward to working with you."

He gave her an easy grin that flashed a glimpse of a dimple. Her mind clouded as she took in his handsome face. She shook her head to clear her thoughts and, before she could reply, he vanished down the hall. And that was exactly why she didn't need to take this case. His mere presence played havoc with her hormones, and she didn't like that one bit.

Sara slumped into her chair and flipped through the playboy's file. Marco had included a copy of the police report and forensic analysis of the crime scene. The victim had sustained one fatal, single bullet wound to the heart. She'd been found by a teacher who happened to be her carpooling buddy. The police had no suspects. She flipped to a photo of the woman. Even though the photo was in color, the victim's face was as white as the sheet covering her body from her feet to her collar bone. Her hair was brown with a hint of red. An ugly yellow-purplish bruise marred her pale face and her bottom lip was split where she'd apparently been hit. Sara unclipped the picture, held it up, and whispered into her empty office, "Who did this to you?"

"That's what we were hired to find out," Lexi answered from the doorway.

Sara sat the picture down and picked up another one to examine as Lexi occupied an empty chair in front of Sara's desk. She picked up the discarded photo. "Are you ready to go?"

"Go where?"

"Your last fitting, remember? I personally added it to the calendar in your cell phone so you wouldn't forget."

"Yeah, just give me a second." Sara glanced down at another photo of the dead woman, taken when she'd been alive. This one showed Mary smiling. Collin was dressed in a suit with his arm draped over her shoulders. She had a quality about her that pulled people in. Sara imagined that Mary would have been an easily likable person, someone Sara would have been friends with. The more she read of the file on the murdered woman, the more determined she became.

"Crap," Sara mumbled while running a hand over her face.

She tossed the photo back into the file and glanced up at Lexi.

"What's the matter?"

Sara released a long sigh. "I just figured out that as much as I hate the idea of pretending to 'date' Collin Martin, I hate the idea of any helpless woman ending up dead over their past mistakes."

Lexi stood and placed the picture back on top of the file. "What makes you think Collin was a mistake? He could actually be a nice guy."

Sara snorted, grabbed her purse, and followed Lexi out. "As if. I bet that man's ego is bigger than your bank account."

Lexi laughed and linked her arm through Sara's as they left the building. "You know how much I'm worth, right?"

Sara leaned into Lexi's arm. "That's exactly my point."

# 3 CHAPTER

After the fitting, Sara went home and scoured Collin's file again. When that didn't give her the answers she needed, she did the next best thing and hopped on the computer, hoping that a few articles might shed some light about her new client. Numerous web pages came up, over three million to be exact, that paid homage to both his hot body and drool-worthy looks. The media had painted the man a damn saint for all of his charity work, and not just any saint…he was being named Humanitarian of the Year by Care Relief, which organizes and helps families dealing with Cancer and other deadly diseases. The man was a saint. "For the love of all that is holy…" She shook her head. "Why me?" Her shoulders sagged in resignation as she amended her complaint. "Why him?"

Rich, powerful, and good looking, this man was a triple threat to whatever sanity she had left.

Sara scratched her head, wondering why more deranged lunatics hadn't emerged from the shadows setting their sights on him.

Newspapers and tabloids had somehow gotten their hands on information about the murder and the letters that had been sent. She pondered how they could have possibly obtained the information. An inside job? The killer himself? Or had Collin or his publicist leaked the information for more publicity? One way or another, she'd find out. She kept reading. To her dismay, with every report and every accusation the lump in her throat grew. The reporters even went as far as to speculate on whether he'd show up to the next fundraiser alone or with a date. She'd fallen asleep with visions of a partially clad Collin, dressed in chaps, with a whip in his hand and a sexy grin on his face.

****

Senator Boyles pounded his fist on the solid oak desk, not concerned about anyone being in the building at such a late hour. His security detail had entered his office only ten minutes ago with the incriminating, career-ending news.

"How in the hell did you let this happen!" he demanded. Styles and Williamson didn't respond; they continued to keep straight faces. It was the worst day of his life and their restraint in showing any emotion just pissed him off worse. The scandal threatened to ruin his re-election campaign. If these pictures made it into the hands of his opponent, then he was screwed, literally and figuratively. Natasha wasn't just his playmate. No, she was much more—the daughter of a fucking congressman. He knew he was playing with fire when he pulled her into his world, but he couldn't stop himself once he'd gotten one sweet taste of the nectar she offered.

So here he was, in the midst of a scandal because of the illicit play. The club had strict rules concerning whom they let into their world. Someone was going to pay for not doing their damn job of screening the applicants. Knowing that even one person had managed to sneak in a camera sent his blood pressure through the roof. It only made sense that an employee had to have been involved. There was no note in the envelope, no return address, nothing to indicate what the photographer might be after.

Senator Boyles opened his desk drawer and pulled out some pink pills for his upset stomach and popped two into his mouth. He rubbed his hand over his bald head, wiping the sweat that had started to form. He was in deep shit and he knew it. He tossed the file to Styles. "Clean this shit up. I want to know who took the pictures; and for you to destroy every copy they made, and silence whoever was involved. If this gets out, I'm ruined."

\*\*\*\*

Sara glanced down at the memory stick she had sitting on top of the pile of prints she'd left in her passenger seat and cursed. She'd meant to put them in her safe at home until she could get Marco the entire package of the senator's escapade with detailed notes of where she'd followed him, when meeting other people in private. It wasn't just about the photos but they were the damning evidence that Marco might need. "Crap."

She pulled through the open iron gates of Collin's estate. No security stopped to ask her why she was there. He had no security period, and that just wasn't going to do. Sara shook her head and mumbled to herself, "Unbelievably naïve. He's going to need additional detail to work security around the perimeter of the property."

The drive to the other side of town hadn't taken as long as she'd thought. His neighborhood was just as she'd imagined; pricey mansions with wrought iron gates around the perimeter. Expensive cars, with probably less than fifty miles on them, sitting idle in the driveways; each homeowner trying to one up the other.

Incredibly large and extremely old oak trees lined and hung over the long driveway to Collin's home, shading visitors as they entered. The surrounding lush green grounds were meticulously cut and well kept. It was a beautiful location. She herself had grown up in a similar home and a similar neighborhood. Of course, her parents had better sense and had a full security detail working the gate. Her father, being assistant deputy director of the FBI, wouldn't have had it any other way. He loved his family, almost to the point of being too protective when she was growing up.

She pulled up into the cobblestone circle drive and parked, taking an extra minute to collect her nerves. This case was similar to the one Lexi had just finished a few months ago, only the big difference was that their best friend, Catherine's, life had hung in the balance. It had been an inside job, and Sara wondered if this one would turn out the same.

She grabbed the memory stick and prints before stepping out of the car. She secured them in the trunk, slammed it shut, and made her way to the large double door entry. Sara ran her fingers over the masterfully carved design on the door. The door swung open before she could even knock. A long-legged blonde stood in the threshold. "You must be Ms. Johnson. We've been expecting you."

It was apparent she wasn't the maid, and something about that observation made Sara pause. Why was a woman like this answering the door at the home of the "world's most eligible bachelor"? Had he mentioned an assistant? A sister? A cousin? Damn, had she missed something in the meeting because she'd been so preoccupied studying his freaking hands?

The woman's hair ran down the length of her back. Hell, even her jeans had creases. I mean, seriously, who has time to iron jeans when there is a perfectly good dryer to throw those babies in to get the wrinkles out. Her button-down shirt was tucked in and secured with an ornate brown belt. This was the type of woman Sara could imagine Collin dating, someone the complete opposite of herself. Blonde and beautiful, probably knew which fork to use with the salad during a meal. Whereas Sara was tall, brunette and tomboyish, nothing like the sophisticated women people probably would expect him to date. The blonde held the door open for Sara to enter and closed it behind her. Blondie's heels clacked against the white marble floors as she walked farther into the showcase home.

Sara crossed through the foyer into a huge spacious room. In the middle, of the elegant room, stood a cherry table holding a vase of several dozen exotic flowers sitting smack dab in the center of it. A floral fragrance that Sara couldn't name drifted openly throughout the room. Everything about this house was perfect almost to the point of OCD. She steeled her hands against the impulse to nudge the vase off center. The foyer opened into a large ballroom type room. However tempted she was to cup her hands and call out to see if her echo would bounce around the room, she didn't. Paintings hung on the stark white walls. People in Lexi's circle of friends would know the names. The dark wood furniture held splashes of deep reds and blues and could have been included in any style magazine. The decor suited his persona, confidence with a splash of style and grace, but was his home an accurate portrait of the person he was or just what he wanted people to believe? Only time would tell.

"And you are?" Sara asked as she shrugged out of her favorite coat, oversized and comfortable, and she'd loved it… until now. Looking at the elegant and poised woman in front of her, Sara realized now that the coat wasn't comfortable. It was downright frumpy. She resolved that she would go coat shopping at her first opportunity. She draped the coat over her arm.

The blonde held out her hand, displaying perfectly manicured pink-painted nails. "I'm Regina Marks, Collin's assistant. It's nice to meet you."

Sara shook the extended hand, embarrassed and hopeful that Regina wouldn't notice her chipped polish. "Sara Johnson, I'm an investigator for Carrington-Hill."

Regina's knowing smile didn't reach her eyes, evident that the blonde had an idea of what was going on. "I know." She gestured for Sara to follow her. "It's a shame Collin has to deal with all of this mess. He's such a nice man."

*That remains to be seen.* Sara congratulated herself. At least she hadn't blurted out her thoughts like she'd done yesterday in the conference room. She'd managed to show a bit more restraint and appeared to be back in control of her mouth. She followed behind Regina, farther into the deep unknown. The assistant glanced back. "Collin's in his study."

"Have you worked for him long?" Sara asked, thinking that now was as good a time as any to get a feel for those that worked close to him. They could offer a wealth of information if she asked the right questions.

"Three months. His publicist, Maureen, hired me." Regina kept talking as she turned the corner that led them down another long hallway. "I mainly just keep his schedule and look after his house. Sometimes I accompany him on his trips but not very often."

Sara had to bite her lip. All kinds of catty comments were running though her mind about

Blondie accompanying Collin on his trips. Mistress and maid, perhaps? Or maybe he liked it both ways? The mistress dressed up like a maid. She held in her snort. She'd witnessed kinkier just from following numerous politicians around town. She stopped in front of a closed door. "Collin is pretty self-sufficient although I have had to remind him to eat a time or two when he gets so engrossed working on the computer that he forgets."

Regina pushed the door open. "Collin, Ms. Johnson has arrived."

Sara heard him grunt even as she walked in. His profile was to them, his fingers flying over the keyboard in a furious pace. His office was large and his mahogany desk was cluttered with papers. A bookshelf stood on one wall, covering every square inch of space. Two supple brown leather chairs sat in front of the oversized desk. A baseball sat on top of his inbox and she could imagine him leaning back in his chair and tossing it in the air while he thought through his problems. The room was welcoming, inviting, and lived in, unlike what she'd seen so far through the rest of his house. This was the space of a man she could be attracted to. She realized this room represented the true Collin Martin, a man who was comfortable and confident, and not the room of an alter ego the media had conjured up. A very thin line ran between the two.

Regina pulled the door closed behind her, leaving Sara with the bachelor who looked extremely busy and downright delectable. His hair was disheveled, as if he'd just slid out of bed. He lifted a hand and ran his fingers through his hair answering her mystery on what might have caused it. She shook her head pushing the crazy thoughts away. They were as bad as when she'd been admiring his hands and look where that had gotten her. "If this is a bad time…"

He didn't even let her finish. "No, have a seat. Just give me one more second."

*Click, click, click.* He leaned back in his chair and sighed. "There, I'm all done."

Collin swiveled from the computer table, on the side of his desk, to face her. He ran a hand over his smooth chin, the same chin that had sported a five o'clock shadow yesterday. The woodsy scent of his aftershave drifted to her nose.

"I hope I didn't interrupt."

Leaning back in the chair, he grinned. "Not at all. I just finished uploading my latest business venture. It's a dating website."

*Ping.*

Sara glanced at the screen. Her posture became rigid as she dug her chipped, painted nails into her palms. "What the hell is that sound?"

He shrugged. "My first client. Each ping represents a single soul looking for their perfect match."

*Ping, ping, ping.* The sound rang through the room; each ping may have been happiness for the person signing up for the services, and maybe even a paycheck for him, but to her, it reminded her of nails screeching down a chalk board. *Ping, ping, ping.*

She gestured toward the computer. "Do you mind turning down the volume? I can hardly hear myself think."

He slid back around in his chair and, a couple clicks later, the obnoxious sound disappeared.

At the mention of the word "dating", she'd tensed. It was one thing to pretend date, but a whole different can of worms to do the real deal. She cleared her throat. "I have some questions about your case."

"Okay."

"Do you have any idea how the press found out about your connection? Any idea who might have leaked the news?"

He shook his head. "No, and before you even ask, I've checked with Regina and my publicist to see if they had anything to do with it. They both said no."

"Who else knew?"

He worried his bottom lip as he thought. "The only other people who knew the connection, were my family… and everyone that lives in my hometown in Virginia." He held up his hands. "And my friend Jim Hanson, the local sheriff here in Kodiak Falls, when I made a report about the mail."

"Why not the FBI?" she inquired.

"Jim said that the FBI wouldn't touch it yet since there was no direct death threat against me. Even the newspaper clipping, that showed my arm around Mary, wasn't a threat. He implied, since there hadn't been a federal crime committed, they would leave it up to the local police to solve."

She nodded, remembering other times when protocol had stopped her father from getting involved. The local authorities were adamant they could handle it as long as no federal lines were crossed and, in Collin's case, no federal crime had occurred. Yet.

"Since you're on a first name basis with the sheriff, I assume you know him well?"

Collin nodded. "We came to be friends about three years ago, and I've been to every fundraiser and benefit he's had since, including the last one just a month ago for his re-election. He is really a good guy."

"Do you own a gun, Mr. Martin?"

He slid the bottom drawer of his desk open and dug around before pulling out a revolver. He laid it on top of the stack of papers between them. He brushed at the dust-covered metal. "Just this one."

She nodded and stood. "Are you licensed to carry a concealed weapon and do you know how to shoot?"

He crossed his arms over his chest and raised a brow, giving her a cocky smile. One she was starting to become familiar with, after working with Garrett for so long.

Oh for the love of god. She hadn't asked the length of his cock or questioned his manhood. She needed to know that, in a jam, he would know how and what to do with a damn gun.

"Yes."

"Good." She had her work cut out for her and she was going to insist on a raise after his job…a big one…and a vacation too. "From now on, you

27

need to keep it on you at all times. I'm also going to recommend placing security at your gate. You don't want to give the murderer free rein of your property."

His jaw ticked, but he nodded just the same. She needed to convey the severity of the situation if she was going to have a shot at keeping them both alive. And losing wasn't an option. Score one for her. Maybe he was going to be easy to train after all. She grinned and held in her chuckle. She'd be doing a public service to women of the world everywhere.

"I also need a list of each of your ex-girlfriends and all of your acquaintances."

He held up his index finger and turned back to the computer. "The ex-girlfriends are easy." He clicked away, pulled up a website, and sent something to his printer. "Marvin Sanchez just did an unofficial expose about my past relationships."

Sara rounded the desk. "Unofficial?"

Collin shrugged. "He's a blogger. There's nothing I could do to stop him."

She pulled the pages from the printer. At the top of the list was a picture of the school teacher with a short bio.

She waved the paper in her hand. "Any of these women have a personal vendetta against you? End any of the relationships on bad terms?"

He took the list and glanced at the three pages. "Only Coleen Boatwright." He glanced up. "I caught her cheating on me and things ended pretty bad, publicly, if you know what I mean." He hitched his thumb over his shoulder back toward the computer. "I believe Marvin has the sound bite on his website if you'd like to listen to it."

Her stomach clenched and she mentally said a silent thanks that her own escapades hadn't been captured to live for eternity on the internet. "Must be hard to live in the limelight, have your whole life on display for the world to see."

He stood. "More pros than cons; it's worth the embarrassment."

She couldn't imagine the so called pros. She shivered thinking of her life being in the media. It was bad enough that they still liked to see if they could find her for an occasional picture, just as they had when she'd left the underground club. Why someone would want in-your-face paparazzi constantly was beyond her. "What makes it worthwhile?"

Collin clasped his hands in front of him. "Because of who I am. I help a lot of medical charities." He shrugged. "I look at it this way. If my face can bring in some extra cash for research, the lack of privacy is a small price to pay for helping since I'm not a doctor able to work on the cures."

Damn it all to hell and back. This man seemed too good to be true. Only time would tell. She spun on her heel and moved over to the door. "Good day, Mr. Martin. I'll be in touch."

"Ms. Johnson."

She plastered a fake smile on her face and turned, unhappy that she hadn't found his flaw yet. "Yes, Mr. Martin?"

He tossed her a key ring with two keys attached. "I figured since we'll be going over lists during the day and going to fundraisers and functions at night, it might be easier on you if you stayed here."

She shook her head and tossed the keys back. "I won't intrude…"

He tossed them back. "The keys are to your own place on the property; I respect your need for privacy. It's not even in the house." He tilted his head toward the wall behind him. "It's a one-bedroom apartment on the other side of the pool. My brother was staying in it, but last night, we moved him into the house."

Her spirits perked up at the mention of his pool. "Your brother lives here?"

He nodded. "He's been staying with me for the last month. He's a little down on his luck and between jobs."

"Any sibling rivalry I need to know about? Any reason to suspect he had anything to do with the murder?"

He pushed from his chair, rounded the desk, and leaned on it. "Ms. Johnson, he's my family. He's not a killer."

Her thoughts went back to her father and how pissed he was going to be that she was not only making herself a target but another spectacle. She reminded herself that it was just for show. She politely nodded and shook the keys. "Thanks."

Regina walked Sara out and handed her some papers along with Sara's frumpy coat. "Since you'll be accompanying Collin to his fundraisers, I thought you might like a copy of his schedule."

"Thanks." Sara walked out of the house and closing her eyes, lifted her head up to the sun, basking in the warmth, wishing she was anywhere doing anything else except getting involved with this man and his problems.

She sighed, hopped in the SUV and tossed the offending coat into the passenger seat. It was a lost cause. There was no crying over assignments. Nope, she'd suck it up and get it over with as fast as possible. Sara had a killer that was standing in her way, preventing her life from returning back to normal.

Sara's brows knit together as a headache formed smack dab between her eyes as she started reading the list. Was it even possible that all of these charity events were happening so close together? The only time she'd ever paid attention to the lifestyle section of the newspaper was to cut out Lexi's engagement announcement. Not once, since she'd been sixteen, had it crossed her mind to consider going to fundraisers and social events. Her father had, thankfully, quit making her go when she'd committed her first faux pas within elite social circles. She'd worn a bright yellow dress to a black and white affair. Sara snickered. Her plan had worked that time. Now she just needed something to get her out of her current situation.

# 4 CHAPTER

Sara drove down Collin's driveway, his very unsecure driveway, and shook her head, thinking of all the work she'd have to put into this one assignment. She turned left toward her house on the other side of town, thinking that maybe if she was lucky the freeway would save her some time.

She hit the Bluetooth on her phone and grinned at the sound of the voice that replied.

"Hey, Sara," Garrett answered on the first ring.

"Hey, G, I need a favor."

He grumbled through the line, but she knew he'd do whatever she needed. They all would. Sara hit the freeway ramp and increased her speed, effectively maneuvering through the somewhat less crowded and faster paced highway compared to the congested streets of downtown.

"What do you need? I hear you've already got a date to Lexi's wedding."

Sara rolled her eyes at the teasing. "Hopefully, I'll be done with this assignment well before the wedding. I need you to run a full background check on..." She didn't finish her sentence when she spotted the SUV riding her bumper in her rearview mirror. "Damn, these people need to learn how to drive."

She moved over to the opposite lane, just to have the vehicle follow. Almost like a well-choreographed dance, they'd moved in tandem three more times. The SUV had followed each time. "He's riding my bumper and won't go around me."

Garrett's voice deepened, as though he'd flipped an instant switch from flirtatious to concern in three seconds flat. "Sara, where are you?"

Sara squinted, trying to read the upcoming sign. "I just left the client's house on I22, and I'm passing exit 4. I'm pretty sure this asshole is a tail. He won't get off my ass even after I move out of the way. I even slowed down, so he knew I wouldn't be the one luring all of the cops out of hiding."

"Get off at the next exit and then get immediately back on the freeway. I'll intercept you." She could hear the rev of Garrett's Corvette through the line.

"Garrett..." She was about to argue, but the vehicle moved closer. "He's kissing my ass, and I'm tempted to hit the brakes."

"Sara," Garrett growled. "Get off at the next ramp."

Sara waited until the very last second before swerving onto the exit ramp, barely missing the guardrail. Her gaze went back and forth between the road in front of her and the SUV following. She'd almost sighed in relief until she heard the screech of the tires.

"They just turned onto the ramp." Sara barely slowed through the yellow light. She cut the wheel to the left and sped to get back on the freeway, going in the opposite direction.

Minutes ticked by before she spotted the SUV again in her rearview mirror, and it was coming in fast.

"Johnson, what's your twenty?" Gone was the playful man who'd answered the phone. Garret was obviously back in agent mode.

"Northbound I22 just passed exit 4, *again*." Sara gripped the wheel tighter and pressed harder on the accelerator. "I don't want to lead them back to Collin's, so I'm going to try and lose them on Main Street. Maybe we can surround them and block them in. They won't even see it coming."

"Negative," she heard Garrett argue. "You'll put too many civilians in harm's way. Bring it down to the warehouse district. I'll have a team waiting, and we can be set up in position in less than five minutes."

Sara squealed and pitched forward as she was rammed from behind. "They hit me," she choked out.

"You need to get your ass out of there. Take the next exit, and I'll meet you halfway."

Sara shook her head and glanced back up into the mirror. A suffocating sensation tightened her throat. "It's a man behind the wheel, but I can't make out his face."

"Sara." She heard the urgency in Garrett's voice. "Hold them off."

The SUV behind her rammed her again. She gritted her teeth and tightened her death grip on the wheel. Cold fury settled in her veins. "The bastard hit me again."

The SUV came up alongside of her, and she instinctively jerked the wheel to the left, ramming the asshole back. She winced and tightened her hold on the wheel hearing the metal crunch on impact. "Not this time, asshole."

She knew it wasn't very smart to play bumper cars with tons of metal but she couldn't contain her chuckle that she'd gotten the upper hand. She'd beat him to the punch.

Her unexpected laugh died in her throat as she noticed the SUV swerve immediately in retaliation. She swerved off the road onto the rock-covered embankment, barely missing the impact. She'd glided her SUV back toward the road when she was hit again.

This time the jarring impact sent her vehicle careening down the slope on the side of the road. Her eyes widened in fear at the trees getting closer by the second. She slammed on her brakes to avoid impact and heard the loud pop of her tire while she struggled to maintain control as she slid through the muddy ground but finally, at the last minute, caught traction. The SUV jerked to a halt.

"I'm on foot," she yelled into the cab even as she threw her door open and started running, for the cover of the trees, with pure determination and a rush of adrenaline. She hadn't had time to grab her cell phone which might have helped her, but she was thankful for the gun tucked securely in her leg holster. She ducked behind the nearest tree with the thickest trunk. *Keep it together, Sara.*

This asshole wasn't going to win. It was either him or her and she wasn't going down without a fight. She whipped the revolver from her ankle holster. She heard the unmistakable loud pop of gunfire even over the roar of the cars speeding by. She ducked. The bullet ricocheted off the tree, sending shards of splintered bark flying toward her arm. Had she had on her frumpy ass coat, it wouldn't have even left a scratch but, as it was, the coat was in her passenger seat.

She heard the curse and didn't wait around to see if he'd make a second shot, a more deadly, accurate, second shot. She jumped up and started running farther into the thick of the forest and brush. Her bare arms were scratched by the extended tree branches, as she did a perfect jeté over a downed tree. Take that Ms. Jennings, proof for her old ballet teacher that she had been paying attention during all of her mandatory lessons as a little girl. She wouldn't stop. Her lungs burned as she pumped her arms and legs, running harder and faster through the squish of the mud beneath her feet.

She heard the wail of the sirens in the distance. "Thank God," she mumbled.

She slowed down and crouched, out of sight, behind an oak tree. Her heartbeat throbbed in her ears as she tried to catch her breath. Steeling her nerves, she gripped the gun, ready to take out anyone who breached her location within fifty yards.

"Sara." She released a sigh when she heard the familiar deep, rumbling voice. She lowered her weapon and stepped out of her hiding spot. Garrett was stalking toward her with purposeful strides. A look of relief swept his face when he spotted her. He tugged her into his brotherly embrace. "You had me worried, kid."

He threw his arm around her shoulder and steered her back to the highway and her abandoned and now beaten-up SUV. "Did you get them?"

He lifted the hand he had resting on her shoulder and glanced at his red, sticky, wet fingertips. "You're hurt."

He stopped walking and turned her gently, lifting her arm for a closer look.

She poked and prodded around the bleeding wound. "I'll live. It's just a scratch."

She shoved her gun back in her holster and stood, taking a moment before they started walking back toward the asphalt and into the chaos that waited.

"Did you get a good look at the driver?"

She shook her head. "No, but they were on my ass from the time I left Collin's until they rammed me off the road." She stepped over the tree she'd vaulted over on her jaunt through the woods. "I don't know if it's related to Collin's stalker or not. Hell it could be in retaliation from the Senator case or any other lunatic from my past with the FBI."

Garrett rubbed the stubble on his square jaw. "Sounds like you might need some help on this one."

**\*\*\*\***

Collin collapsed back into his chair and tossed his trusty baseball in the air. Having to rehash his past always made him cringe and, even more so, now that his decisions were being dissected under a microscope. He wasn't a womanizer. There had been only a handful of relationships that lasted longer than a year. He growled in frustration, not knowing how to stop this asshole.

"Tough day?"

He glanced up to find Regina leaning against the doorframe with her arms crossed over her chest and the mail tucked underneath her arm. "You could say that."

Regina sauntered into his office and plopped the mail into his inbox. "I gave Ms. Johnson your itinerary so she knows what she's getting into."

Having Sara around should have eased his mind about finding the killer, but the thought of making her a target was slowly gnawing away at his conscience and eating at his very soul. Putting another woman in danger, even if she was capable of protecting herself, was a crazy idea. What the hell had he been thinking? "Thanks. I gave her the keys to the pool house and an extra key to the main house, so you'll probably be seeing more of her."

Collin picked up the mail and started flipping through it.

"You know…she's not really your type. You prefer blondes. Do you think the press is going to buy into the charade?"

Her uncanny regard for speaking the truth, no matter the consequences, was exactly why he'd agreed to keep her on after Maureen had hired her. It was refreshing and welcome, even if her statements sometimes gave him pause.

"I didn't realize I had a type." He set the mail down on his desk, overwhelmed with the unfamiliar need to defend himself against having a specific type. There was nothing wrong with the investigator. He would have taken her out on a date, if he'd come across her under different circumstances. "She's attractive, smart, and knows how to shoot a gun. What's not to like?"

Regina walked back over to the door and paused. She glanced over her shoulder. "Exactly my point, Collin. She carries a gun. I'm just worried about you. If she's a good actress, I don't want you to forget the real reason she's here. I'm saying this as your friend."

Over the last three months, Regina had become more than an assistant. She was his friend, and he confided in her more than his own brother. It was sweet that she was concerned, even if it was unfounded. "The relationship is just a ruse, Regina. Nothing more."

Regina nodded. "I know." She cleared her throat, masked the concern on her face, and turned from friend back into assistant so fast it would have given many whiplash, but not him…he was used to it now. "I'll make sure she has the appropriate attire for your engagements and see that she has everything else she needs."

Collin relaxed into his chair, knowing that Regina would make sure that Sara was taken care of. "Thanks for your help. I really appreciate it."

She tapped on the side of the doorframe. "Anytime, boss."

Regina disappeared, and Collin turned back toward his computer and started accessing the files for all of his colleagues, acquaintances, and friends that Sara had asked for. He let his mind get lost in preparing a spreadsheet that incorporated every known name, email address, phone number, and home address that he had at his disposal. He kept himself submerged in the busy work to help drown out the events that had plagued him for the last month.

He glanced at the time on his computer, surprised to find that three hours had passed. He yawned, pushed to his feet, and raised his arms above his head to stretch his dormant muscles. An angry growl emanated from his stomach, filling the silent room. He'd forgotten to eat, yet again. Collin eyed the gun on the desk. A gun he'd only bought and knew how to use but never thought he might need. It was always just a precaution. Remembering Sara's request to keep it on him at all times, he grabbed the gun and moved through the empty, silent house to the kitchen. He made himself a quick sandwich and retreated to his room where he finished eating and would spend another sleepless night worrying about things he couldn't control.

His head had just hit the pillow and he'd closed his eyes when his cell on the bedside table vibrated. He glanced at the screen and didn't recognize the number, but he answered anyway. "Hello."

Silence greeted him on the other end.

"Hello," he repeated. The silence unnerved him. He tightened the grip on his phone and sat up, leaning against his bed frame. He glanced at the dresser next to him where the revolver rested within reach. A jolt of apprehension fired through his veins, instantly erasing the need to sleep he'd felt only moments ago.

"What? Nothing to say?" He tried baiting the caller, hoping that, if he or she talked, he might recognize a voice, anything that might put an end to the nightmare or prove to him that it was just a prank caller. Even with an unlisted number, he still managed to get anonymous calls every so often from women pledging their undying love.

The person hung up without uttering a single syllable.

Collin woke early the next morning to the blare of his alarm clock. He reached for it and slammed his palm on the snooze button before he even glanced at the time. The calls had continued throughout the night. Each one had given him hope that the person might eventually talk. He'd eventually turned the damn thing off at three in the morning, hoping for at least a few hours of peaceful sleep. He rolled out of the bed, still half asleep, pulled on his favorite cotton sleep pants, bypassed his T-shirt, and then headed for the door. He was going to need coffee today and lots of it if he had any plans of functioning and thinking straight.

Wiping the sleep from his eyes, he hit the start button on the coffee pot and grabbed a mug. His brother, Drew, back from his early morning run, was leaning against the counter in his sweat-soaked shirt, sipping his orange juice.

"Late night?"

"I worked till the wee hours of the morning trying to pull all the information Sara needed to start her investigation and, when I tried to go to bed, I kept getting phone calls, probably just another round of pranks."

"I take it Sara is the investigator you mentioned you were going to see."

Collin nodded.

"Is this Sara chick a curvy brunette with a hot little body?"

"How do you know what she looks like? Did you see her yesterday?"

Drew shook his head and lifted his cup toward the row of windows that overlooked the pool. "I'm guessing that's her."

Glancing out the window, Collin looked beyond the pool until he spotted her. Sara had a black bag strung across her chest and a can of coffee snuggled in the crook of one arm while she dragged a suitcase, with her other hand, toward the pool house. By the looks of it, the suitcase was winning in the fight.

"Looks like she could use a hand. Maybe I should go offer."

Collin grabbed another mug and filled them both. "She's not a new toy, Drew. She's here to do a job, so keep it in your pants."

Without waiting for a reply, Collin stepped out onto the patio and walked over to where she stood jamming the key into the lock.

"Looks like you could use some help." He handed her one of the mugs and slid his other hand over hers. Then he wiggled the key and turned it until he heard the unmistakable click. "It's takes a bit of finesse to get it just right."

Sara let out a sigh and took a sip of her coffee. A stain of scarlet appeared on her cheeks. "I decided to take you up on your offer."

He turned to find her assessing gaze going down the length of his body. A quick big grin stretched his lips, and her face reddened. Yes, doll, you're busted. "Do I pass?"

"Excuse me?"

He stepped toward her and leaned into her ear as he reached behind her for the bag she'd been struggling with. The scent of roses in the afternoon sun drifted to his nose, and he inhaled before he whispered. "Am I your type?"

He heard her breath hitch and grinned, silently wondering if he could make her breath hitch again. He grabbed the bag behind her and straightened. Her pretty red blush was replaced with a scowl. He carried the bag inside and to the bedroom, where he left it on the bed and returned to her moments later.

"I guess you'll do."

He chuckled. "That bag must have weighed a hundred pounds." He motioned toward the coffee can in her hand. Even though it looked imported, he couldn't help his reply. "You know, we have coffee here."

"Not like this," she said over her shoulder as she shrugged out of her coat and tossed it on a nearby chair. She continued to move throughout the small room, testing the locks on the door and the windows. Her face was clouded with unease. "You're in dire need of better security."

She pulled the phone from her pocket, dialed, and placed it against her ear. "Marco, you need to send in the security techs for a major overhaul." She walked back outside and glanced around the doorframe before entering again. "He's going to need alarms and cameras, just for starters, and I'd suggest sending someone you trust to work the gate until this is over."

Sara stopped in her tracks as she listened. "What? When? Did they take anything?" she asked.

That didn't sound good. He whispered, "Was there a break-in?"

She nodded and covered the phone with her palm. "Yeah, someone tried to break into our offices but I think our security scared them off."

More seconds ticked by as she intently listened to whatever Marco was telling her. Finally she released an audible sigh and went back to giving Marco her demands.

This was the first time he was seeing Sara in action, taking over like a woman on a mission, and damn if it wasn't sexy as hell. Her cheeks were flushed; her tiny hands touched everything in her path. He supposed she was right, perplexed why he hadn't considered his security before. The killer hadn't threatened to kill him, only his past girlfriends, but he should have figured that it was better to be safe and alive than sorry and six feet under.

While she paced in front of him, it gave him more time to study her. Her long brown wavy locks swung around her arms with each turn, covering a white bandage attached to her bicep. Her long legs ate up the tiny living room in six steps before she was turning again. The curve of her jeans emphasized her perfectly tight ass, and the slight muscle definition on her arms confirmed that she took good care of herself and possibly even worked out. Her almond-shaped bright blue eyes were outlined by long, thick, black lashes and twinkled every time she made another demand. He didn't have to guess that she enjoyed being the one in charge. No, he was starting to understand her type. Demanding almost to a fault; calculating and wanting to get her way. Granted, it was for his protection, but he could just imagine how she would be when he showed up with her on his arm to one of the benefits. He instantly knew they were going to have issues.

She stopped pacing and listened intently, all the while chewing on her bottom lip. She mumbled yes a few times, then grumbled, "I'm here for the duration."

She shook her head as though Marco could see her. "I know, but it has to be done if we want to deal with his situation thoroughly and efficiently." She stiffened, turned her back to him, and lowered her voice. "I know he isn't going to like it. Have Lexi explain it to him. He's just going to have to deal with it."

Ending the call, she turned around and lifted the coffee cup to her lips and sipped. "Thanks for the coffee."

Boyfriend? Fiancé'? Or was she talking about her husband like that? He opened his mouth to reply and snapped it closed. He nodded, spun on his heel and stormed out of the guest house. It wasn't the politest thing to do but, he was afraid if he said what was really bothering him, that she might just up and quit. She hurried up behind him as he rounded the pool and grabbed his arm before he could escape the confusing woman who made him rock hard and equally frustrated.

"What's wrong?"

He lowered his head and took a deep breath before his gaze met hers. "Marco never said one way or the other if you were single, only that you were his choice for my situation. It never even dawned on me that you might be in a relationship."

Her lips thinned in irritation; her stance turned guarded. "Why would it matter? I'm here for appearances, not the real thing."

"Either way you look at it doll, how do you think it's going to reflect on me, or yourself for that matter, that my *girlfriend* is in another relationship. Cause let's face it….the press wouldn't have to dig too far to find out the truth if there were a marriage certificate."

Oh, he'd pressed her button all right. Not only did Sara like to be in charge, but she didn't like anyone questioning her judgment to work his case. His jaw twitched as he threw caution to the wind and just blurted out what was really on his mind. "Don't you think you would be a little jealous seeing your boyfriend hugged up all over another woman in magazines and newspaper articles, even if he claimed nothing was going on and it was just for work?"

She threw her head back and laughed; and was that a snort he'd just heard? He crossed his arms over his chest and narrowed his eyes. When she came up for air, she covered her mouth. "Sorry, but you never struck me as the jealous type." She cleared her throat and tried unsuccessfully to mask the smile still on her lips. "I'm single, as in not dating, as in…no one to get jealous."

He pointed to the pool house. "But I heard you say…"

She nodded slowly, as if just catching on to what he meant.

"I wanted Lexi to explain what was going on to my father, not a boyfriend, and definitely not a husband. It's only a matter of time before my dad sees pictures of us together and, trust me when I tell you, you don't want him on your ass."

"Why? Who's your dad?"

\*\*\*\*

Okay, so maybe it wasn't professional to laugh in her client's face, but damn, he was funny. Sara tried to cover up the humor she felt at his statement and failed miserably. "Assistant Deputy Director of the FBI." She shrugged. "You know how it can be with overprotective fathers."

She watched his Adam's apple bob as he swallowed. Yep, he was getting the picture...finally. "He doesn't like it when I make the headlines, and with you..." She motioned up and down his half-clad body. "...we're going to be in the headlines. I just wanted Lexi to give him a heads-up. If I didn't, he'd start with a full background check, and you don't want the FBI in your business. Do you?"

He moved his head from side to side as if releasing the tension in his neck. "I just assumed..."

She waved her hand and rocked back and forth on her heels. "Forget it, just next time ask so you don't go getting yourself worked up over nothing. I'll be straight with you."

He nodded his agreement. "Once you get settled, I'll meet you in my office. I have that other list you asked for. I'm just going to take a quick shower, and I'll be down."

Her imagination was immediately bombarded with images of streams of water gliding down his tall, muscular body. Now if she could just keep herself from inappropriately groping him while managing to keep her eye on the job, she'd be just fine. *Arm's length*, she reminded herself. She turned and started walking back to the pool house. She lifted her hand and wiggled her fingers. "Have fun."

# 5 CHAPTER

Thirty minutes later, she was standing in the doorway to Collin's office and silently watching as he thumbed through his mail, sorting the letters into piles. She felt like she had that night at the exclusive club, a voyeur of sorts trespassing into someone's personal space.

"You must be the investigator," a deep voice said from behind her.

She turned to find a man with Collin's facial features staring back at her. "You must be the brother."

He extended his hand. "Drew Martin, the youngest and better looking of the Martin clan."

"Sara Johnson." She chuckled and shook his hand. The similar characteristics between the brothers were uncanny. High cheekbones, tanned skin, and the brightest, clearest eyes; eyes that could see clear down to your soul. Drew's eye color, however, was more of an ocean green versus the vibrant blue of Collin's eyes. He had a baby face, where the lines on Collin's face were much more defined. She'd bet women would find him as equally deliciously appealing as his brother and maybe even a bit more charming.

She turned to find Collin watching her with his brow hitched. "Knock it off, Drew. She could probably kill you with her bare hands and knows more than a hundred different ways to hurt you."

Drew's voice was velvety smooth and yet playful at the same time. "That sounds sexy and promising." Oh, yeah, he was a definite heartbreaker.

Drew threw his arm over her shoulders. "Don't worry, babe. My heart is already spoken for but, if things don't work out the way I plan, you're moving to the top of my list."

Collin's brows furrowed farther as he shook his head and glanced back down at the mail he had left in his hands. His whole demeanor did a one-eighty right in front of her. He abruptly stood, sending the chair whirling into the wall behind him. Blood drained from his face, and the rise and fall of his chest quickened. He dropped the rest of the mail on his desk and held up an envelope, just like the ones he'd shown her that day at the office. She wasn't quick enough to stop him from tearing into the envelope and pulling out the paper, so she rounded the desk, moving to his side to read over his shoulder. And there goes any fingerprint evidence she might have been able to collect. It was now contaminated and probably smeared. She let out an aggravated sigh. "From now on, I'll be collecting your mail and going through it before anyone else touches it."

The letter was like the first one. Each individual letter and word was cut from a magazine and glued into place. "I warned you. Number 2." He flipped to the next page and his hand flew to his mouth. His eyes burned with fury as he tightened his hold on the paper, crinkling it in his hand. She took the paper from him. Printed on the paper was a grainy picture of Collin and a blonde sitting in a coffee shop deep in conversation. An icy chill skirted down her spine.

"Who is she?" Sara asked while studying the photo.

"Tonya."

"Your old girlfriend Tonya? She was one fine specimen. I'll never understand why you two split up," Drew said still standing at the door.

She ignored the comments from the peanut gallery, flipped the paper over, noticed it was blank, and flipped it back to study the innocent picture. She looked for any signs to indicate the two might be together. They weren't holding hands; they were barely smiling. Almost as if they were two strangers on a first date. "When was this taken?"

She glanced up to notice Drew was no longer standing in the doorway. He'd probably left, bored that she was no longer paying him a lick of attention. "A week ago. I ran into her on Main Street." His gaze was still riveted to the picture. His features had now turned to stone.

She noticed the moment his eyes started to glaze and snapped her fingers. "I need you to focus, Collin."

He nodded, and a determination settled in his eyes.

"How do you know her?"

"We dated. The breakup was mutual. She didn't like her life being under a microscope, and I wouldn't give up all my charity work for her. We went our separate ways." He pointed down at the paper. "That was the first time I'd run into her in the last five years. She told me she was about to move in with her boyfriend and they were getting married."

Collin ran his hands through his hair and pulled on the strands. He squeezed his eyes closed. It was evident guilt and anger were prodding at his resolve.

"Do you know where she lives?"

His eyes snapped open, and his brows dipped. "Yeah, if she hasn't already moved in with the boyfriend." He rattled off the address. "Do you think there's a chance she's still alive?"

It was highly unlikely, but she didn't have the heart to tell him that. Not yet, not without knowing for sure. Sara grabbed her phone, fished her keys from her pocket, and spun on her heel. "I don't know."

Dread settled in her gut as she ran from the mansion and hopped in her SUV. Her passenger door jerked open and Collin climbed in. "What do you think you're doing? You need to stay here!"

He pointed down the drive. "You're wasting time. She might still be alive."

She threw the SUV in gear, grabbed the printout of the exposé he'd given her yesterday from the glove box, and handed it to him. "Tell me what numbers Tonya and the teacher are listed as."

He shuffled the papers. "One and four, why?"

She pounded her palm against the steering wheel. Nothing made sense, even the order of the kills was out of sync. "I'm trying to figure out the killer's pattern."

She punched the Bluetooth in her car, informed Marco what was going on, and she asked him to send a team.

Sara skidded around the next curve and punched the gas. She glanced at him. "Why did the killer skip two and three? What is the connection between one and four versus two and three?"

He glanced down at the papers, and she returned her attention back to the road, waiting patiently for him to figure it out. He would be the only one able to connect the pieces. If she pressured him the strain alone might block his reasoning. With wide eyes and his mouth parted, he looked up. "I saw both of them this month."

She nodded toward the paper. "Who else have you seen on that list in the last thirty days?"

He furrowed his brow as he again went through the faces and names of all of his exes. He pointed at number seven. "Amada George." He glanced up. "I ran into her at a fundraiser."

She skidded to a stop at Tonya's address. The high-rise was ten stories tall, and the street was unusually quiet. She pulled out her phone. "What's Amanda's address?"

When he'd told her, she text Amanda's name and address to Lexi and asked her to pick Amanda up and move her to a safe house. Maybe they could prevent or at least slow down the killer since they now had somewhat of a reasoning behind why the killer was only choosing some of the exes and not all of them. She threw open the glove box, grabbed her Beretta and hopped out of the SUV and ran up to the building entrance. Collin was right behind her. "Collin, you need to go wait in the SUV."

He shook his head. "Not on your life."

She reached down and pulled the revolver out of her ankle holster and handed it to him. "There is no safety on this gun, so try not to shoot me."

He nodded. She took the stairs two at a time until they reached the second floor, completely bypassing the elevator. She glanced through the little glass window of the exit door, to ensure the coast was clear, before she pulled it open. They hurried down to the door, and she laid her hand on his arm to stop him. She pushed him so his back was pressed against the wall and motioned for him to wait.

There was no sign of forced entry, no signs of foul play in the hall, so she did the only thing she could. She knocked. No answer. She rang the doorbell. Still no answer.

Movement at the end of the stairwell caught her eye, and she breathed a sigh of relief. Marco, Vickers, and a blonde woman she hadn't seen before were headed her way, each with guns drawn.

This wasn't the time to figure out who the woman was. Introductions would have to wait.

"No one answered," she whispered.

Marco nodded, got down on one knee, pulled a tool from his back pocket, and silently picked the lock. It would have been easier just to kick the damn thing down, which she'd been about to try before Marco arrived. With her luck she'd hurt her leg, the door would have been one of those heavy metal fireproof doors.

He grabbed his gun, straightened, and pushed the door open. It creaked, and she inwardly cringed. *So much for the element of surprise.* She and the team moved, using hand signals as they cleared the living room and kitchen and proceeded down the hall.

The acrid smell of blood and decaying body hit them all at the same time. She glanced back to find Collin had covered his nose and mouth with his shirt. A tear slipped from his lid. He didn't need to see what she knew was on the other side of the door. She turned and pulled him back out into the open living room while the team advanced.

Minutes ticked by as Collin and she waited on the couch for confirmation that it was indeed too late. He sat with his elbows propped on his knees, his head in his hands. Her heart ached for him. No one needed to go through this. The self-blame alone would destroy lesser men.

Sara stood and started to move throughout the room with nervous energy. Boxes had been shoved up against walls, all labeled with room names. She moved to the bar that separated the kitchen from the living room. Unopened mail sat on the counter. She noticed the light blinking on the answering machine, a message that would undoubtedly be left unanswered.

Sara glanced over her shoulder as she pulled her long-sleeve shirt down to cover her fingers and pressed play.

A sweet voice filled the silent room. *"You've missed me, so either leave a message or try me on my cell. If you're a telemarketer, don't bother."*

A hand clamped down on Sara's shoulder, and she jumped. He leaned in closer to the recorder, listening to the silence, waiting to hear a message, trying to find a clue when there wasn't one to find. The machine recorded nothing but silence until the blaring sound of a disconnected call came on.

"I got a call like that."

She spun around. "When?"

"The night before last, right before you moved in."

"Are you insane? You didn't think that little bit of information might be important. Do you have a freaking death wish?"

Sara clenched her hands together to stop from smacking him upside the head. Too bad she couldn't stop her quick tongue from brandishing him like a child. Her comment wasn't very professional. It reminded her of something her father would do, something he would say. And the thought churned her stomach. She stepped toward him. He stepped back. "I'm sorry, Collin, but you have to tell me stuff like that. Even if you think it doesn't mean anything."

He moved back to the couch and plopped down. Damn, she needed to see a doctor, one that could prescribe a drug to stop crap from flying out of her mouth before alienating everyone she'd ever known.

Marco emerged, the stress lines of his face deepening as he pressed the phone to his ear. "One of mine will bring him in. She's also undercover as his current girlfriend, so I'd appreciate it if you kept her employment to yourself for the time being." He clipped the phone closed and shoved it back in his pocket.

Marco nodded with worry in his eyes. She stood and followed him out into the empty hallway. She didn't have to ask if Tonya was dead. She could see it in his face. "You need to take Collin down to the sheriff's office. I've informed the sheriff of what we found and they want to question him. They're sending in their own forensic team to canvas the apartment."

In a soft voice, one he rarely used, he asked, "You do know what this means, don't you?"

"He was right. His exes are being targeted for extermination and the killer is most likely a stalker." She knew exactly what this meant. As if trying to catch a murderer wasn't bad enough, Collin's murderer was also a damn stalker, monitoring and following his every move, and that knowledge changed everything.

His brows dipped. "Most of the time stalkers only become violent when they are frustrated and start realizing the object of their affection doesn't want them. I'm thinking either sociopathic or schizophrenic. Hell, it could be a combination of both. We don't know what the hell we're dealing with" He turned and paced a few steps away and back. "We have to figure out what set the stalker off, why she or he feels threatened by his exes."

She placed a reassuring palm on his arm. "He'd seen both of them within the last month. I'm thinking that this psycho has targeted him within that time frame. I think we need to retrace his steps over the last thirty days. He's only seen one other ex since then, and I've texted Lexi and asked her to pick up and move Amanda George into a safe house for the time being until we get this figured out."

He grinned. "I always knew you were smart." He walked back over to the apartment door. Sara laid a hand on his arm to stop him. "He's gotten phone calls in the middle of the night." She tilted her head toward the apartment door. "Just like the one I heard on Tonya's machine while I was waiting for you. Someone called started breathing heavy and hanging up. It might be worth pulling the records and tapping his line." Marco winked and grinned before pushing open the door and walking back inside. "You need to get him out of here before the press shows up. I'm sure they'll catch wind of this on the police scanners."

Sara followed Marco back into the apartment and placed a gentle hand on Collin's shoulder. "We've got to go down to the station, Collin. The sheriff needs to take your statement."

He looked up with red-rimmed eyes and nodded. And that pissed her off more. Gone was the playboy she'd read about in the tabloids, replaced with a man that cared.

"No, no, no. No crying on my watch."

She sat down facing him and grabbed his hand. "I promise you this person is going down. I'll hunt him or her down, and I promise to make it hurt."

He squeezed her hand before pulling her off the couch. "Let's get this over with."

She needed to get him out of there before the media showed up or, worse, the killer. They needed a game plan, one that ended with him staying alive and Sara throwing this asshole in jail.

# 6 CHAPTER

Sara pulled into a parking spot in the garage at the sheriff's department, a place she'd visited plenty of times while working for the FBI. There was a high probability that people would recognize her and her cover would be blown. She pulled the keys from the ignition and turned in her seat. "Okay, this is how we're going to play this."

He sat dazed as he stared out of the windshield. Unsure if he'd even heard her, she reached for his hand and slid her fingers through his. The physical contact was intimate and worked exactly like she'd wanted it to. He glanced down at their joined hands before his eyes met hers.

"They are going to ask you questions about how you knew Tonya and what we were doing there to find the body. Just be honest. Tell them about the letter you received and remind them that you've already filed a report."

"I'm sorry I dragged you into my drama. If you want to back out, I'll understand." He lightly squeezed her hand. His words were a mere whisper in the quiet of the car. He was somber and quiet as though his life was being sucked right out of him; he was nothing like the man she'd met a few days ago.

Sliding her fingers from his, she opened the door. "Not on your life, not until this is over. Come on. Let's get this over with, and then we can get back to finding this asshole."

He got out of the car and started walking toward the door. He grabbed her hand and kissed the inside of her wrist. His action made her stumble over her own two feet, but she quickly righted herself. He held up their entwined fingers. "Appearances."

The butterflies in her stomach ravished her from the inside out and twisted into tiny knots, making her heartbeat work double time. Something as simple as holding the man's hand turned her into a clumsy idiot. What the hell was wrong with her? *Get a freakin' grip. Appearances*, she reminded herself. That was the whole reason she was there. She hoped the mental pep talk would get her through the next few weeks because being in this close proximity to him was leaving her in a constant state of sexual frustration. One that threatened to send her into a tailspin, and she refused to go down in a ball of flames.

His hold on her hand tightened as they made their way to the front desk. Half of the lobby was occupied by people in chairs. There was a woman weeping into her palms while a man sat next to her rubbing her back. Phones down the hall rang several times before she heard them answered. Men in green uniforms and badges walked by, sipping from mugs. The scent of coffee permeated the air around her. The place was orderly, unlike the probable scenes from the night before when the criminals had been arrested and cuffed.

A woman with blinding, bleached blonde hair was poised behind the counter, with the phone pressed to her ear while she picked and played with her pink gum. Wow, where was Sara's sunglasses when she needed them. The woman glanced up and grinned as she set the phone back into the cradle.

Little Miss Sunshine stood up, and her eyes lit up like a woman given the best, most expensive box of chocolates on Valentine's Day. If Sara hadn't been there, Collin would have been fresh meat, and that was sooo not happening. Not today, not with her. "Collin, it's nice to see you again."

Collin glanced down at Sara. His brows knit together, and he squeezed her hand. "Uh...you too."

Sara smiled and playfully batted Collin's arm. "Well, honey, aren't you going to introduce us?" She held out her hand to the twit that had eyes on her client. "I'm Sara Johnson."

A dark brown brow hitched into her white bangs. The fake blonde glanced between both of them and then down at Sara's hand before she took it and shook.

KATE ALLENTON

"I'm Katrina." She beamed a big white smile as she glanced over at Collin. "I didn't know you were dating anyone. You should have brought her to the last fundraiser. I'm sure mom would have loved to meet her."

*Huh.* Sara let her hand drop, leaned over the desk, and tapped the surface. "Can you tell the Sheriff that we're here? He's expecting us."

Katrina kept her smile as she picked up the phone and announced them. Awkward silent seconds ticked by as Collin threw his arm over Sara's shoulders and steered her away from the desk. When out of the woman's earshot, she whispered, "Please tell me she isn't another ex."

He leaned down and whispered in her ear. The move would appear to onlookers that he was kissing her cheek. "She looks familiar but, honestly, I have no idea who she is."

Sara giggled and leaned farther into his arms to give any onlookers a good show. The more people thought they were a couple, the quicker they could draw the killer out into the open.

The door to the station burst open. A well-dressed older gentleman, wearing a business suit and tie walked in. He was followed by two huge men dressed in black with comms pressed in their ears, the kind with the black coiled wires disappearing into the back of their coats. The men reminded Sara of the Secret Service agents that would follow behind the president or other high public officials.

One of them turned to look behind him, and she noticed the gun and immediately stepped in front of

Collin blocking him from the unknown. Security detail or not, they had a weapon, and she didn't have any idea who the hell they were.

"Congressmen Benton?"

The well-dressed yet, somewhat, frazzled man turned toward the sound of Collin's voice and stepped forward with an extended hand. "Collin, this is a surprise. I hope you're just visiting someone you know and not in any sort of trouble."

Collin put his arm around Sara's shoulders. "I could say the same for you…what brings you down to the sheriff's office? I wasn't even aware you were in town."

The congressman frowned and his shoulders sagged in defeat. "Natasha came here on vacation and didn't return home. We've been trying to call her for the last forty-eight hours with no luck."

The congressman's eyes were bloodshot with bags sagging beneath; he was clearly out of sorts and worried about his daughter.

Collin patted the congressman on the back. "We both know how Natasha is. I'm sure she just met up with some friends and lost track of time."

The deep lines on the Congressman's forehead didn't ease. Collin's words did little to lighten the worry still present in the official's eyes. One of bodyguards motioned the congressman down the hall. They turned into an office and out of sight.

Sara leaned into Collin and whispered, "You didn't date her too, did you?"

Collin shook his head. "No, Natasha was a bit too wild for my taste, although that didn't stop her from trying to hook up with me every time we saw each other."

Sara plopped down in one of the hard chairs to wait as he continued to stand in front of her, giving her a view of the bulge behind his zipper. Packs to the left and from the looks of it, he was a bit turned on too. She instinctively licked her lips and glanced up at him.

He winked, leaned down and placed a quick kiss on her lips. For the love of god, she'd been busted again, not very stealthy of her, and not really the ideal place for her to have been looking. She was in a police station to give a statement about a murder, and what did she have on her mind? Sex, yep, leave it to her to pick the most inappropriate times for her libido to kick in and take notice.

He brought out the worst in her. Her thoughts had been deep in the gutter since she'd met him. If she wasn't busy laughing at him, she'd been busy undressing him with her mind. Her cheeks felt red hot, like even an ice cube couldn't cool them down. Damn man. Flustered, she glanced up. "How do you know him?"

Collin slid into the seat next to hers. "I met him several years ago at a fundraiser, and we've been friends ever since."

She didn't have time to dig deeper before they were interrupted as a muscular man with a holster strapped to his broad shoulders headed in their direction. He had short salt-and-pepper hair and an air of authority. The Sheriff, if she had to guess. He extended his hand. Collin took her elbow and pulled her to her feet.

"Collin, it's good to see you again. I just wish it was under different circumstances."

Collin removed his arm from around her shoulder and shook the man's hand. "Sheriff."

Okay, so maybe the way the sheriff carried himself wasn't because of the big guns he had strapped to his body. The man was all about business, hardly sparing time for pleasantries, and somewhat reminded Sara of her father. The sheriff turned and motioned them to follow him down the hall. The scent of coffee got stronger, almost making her salivate. The banter between two cops at a water cooler ceased as they passed. "We just need to get an official report."

They all walked in silence, turning and filing into the cluttered office at the end of the hall. The white plastered walls were littered with commendations and pictures. A younger version of the blonde, only with dark hair, was in most of them. Sara pointed with her thumb back to his door. "Is the blonde at the front desk your daughter?"

He nodded. "That's Katrina, my oldest. She's covering for Martha while she's on maternity leave. This is only a temporary gig until she finds another job, one more suitable to her liking."

Collin crossed one ankle over his other leg. "That explains it. I knew she looked familiar, but she wasn't blonde at the benefit. She was a brunette back then, wasn't she?"

The sheriff shrugged. "It's possible; she changes her hair color when the wind blows. The whole family was there."

Collin nodded, dismissing the information, and they got down to business. He explained about the letter and the reason they'd gone to Tonya's apartment. He also explained that he'd bumped into her one week prior. Sara interrupted and explained her theory about the murderer probably also being a stalker and that Carrington Hill Investigations was in the process of moving another one of Collin's exes to a secure location just to keep her safe. After an exhausting hour of rehashing the events from the last two days, they all said their goodbyes. The sheriff told Collin not to leave town without notifying him and that he'd call if he had any more questions or information. The sheriff's down-to-business demeanor and series of questions were enlightening, instantly telling her from the way the questions were worded that Collin wasn't a suspect.

They arrived back at Collin's house and headed inside just as the sun was starting to set on the horizon. Her mind was running ninety to nothing with all of the questions she needed to ask him, questions that she shouldn't put off any longer. If that meant she was going to be cooped up with him in his study, she had some frustrations to work out before they talked. She walked into the kitchen and started the coffee maker as he slid into one of the stools on the other side of the bar. "Is your pool heated?"

"Yeah, it's a consistent eighty degrees. Why?" Collin asked as he rubbed his neck.

"We need to come up with a plan, and I do my best thinking while I'm swimming laps. How about we meet in your office in about an hour?"

He flashed her one of his dimples and her mind went immediately to trying to figure out if she could make him flash her both. Yet, another reminder why she needed the time alone. Not just to think about his case, but to douse her hormones to get them back under control. The indentation in his cheek deepened.

"Sure, my office in an hour." He stood and walked out of the kitchen, leaving her alone to finish making her coffee. Then she planned to go back to the pool house and change into her bathing suit.

She slipped into a white fluffy cotton robe and stepped out onto the patio. The moonlight glistened off the water in the heated oversized pool. Stars twinkled high in the night sky. Even though it was a brisk October, the heated pool and a night swim promised to relieve the knots that had taken up permanent residence in her shoulders ever since she'd met the un-dateable bachelor. For the next hour, she would submerge herself into her workout, a surefire way to bring a little bit of sanity and rational thinking back into her overactive imagination and uncontrollable desires. She only hoped that neither Collin nor Drew would appear thinking that she'd want the company, because she didn't.

She set her phone on the patio table, untied the sash of her robe, and slid out of the warm material before draping it over a nearby chair and stepping down into the warm water. It was a nice contrast from the cool night air. The smell of fresh-cut grass drifted on the slight breeze. She stepped off the last step and dunked her head, submerging her body into the welcoming arms of the familiar routine. She ran her hands over her head and wiped the water from her eyes to find Collin standing by the table where she'd left her phone.

"Hope you don't mind." He set his beer down along with the extra one he had in his hand and untied his robe, leaving it draped over the back of the patio chair next to hers. His perfectly muscled body had been kissed by the sun. The muscles in his arms tightened as he picked up his beer and took a big swig. She stood there like an idiot and admired the man standing before her. He was the epitome of perfection. Everything about him oozed sex appeal, drawing unsuspecting women to him like a moth to a flame. He leaned over dropping the robe on the chair flexing his abs.

"I could bounce a quarter off those babies." Her hand flew to her mouth as her eyes widened. She couldn't believe she'd said that out loud.

His deep chuckle filled the air, only to be drowned out by Sara submerging herself in the water, hoping when she came up for air that he'd be gone. Another minute went by before she broke the surface. No such luck, he was still there.

"You could try."

She groaned, ducked underwater again, and kicked to the shallow end of the pool. She pushed off the wall and swam under water before submerging with strokes to swim the full length of the pool and back again eight times before she stopped to catch her breath.

\*\*\*\*

Sara was definitely a hard woman to figure out. He'd never had to work so hard for a woman's attention. Too bad she never acted on the comments she blurted out. What was the matter with him? Collin leaned back against the steps and sipped his beer as he watched Sara push herself to the brink of exhaustion. The white bandage on her arm was now soaked through. She had to stop sometime to catch her breath, didn't she? He chuckled and then waited for her to come up for air. She finally came up and inhaled several big breaths, her chest quickly rising and falling as her lungs fought to refill with air.

"You always push yourself like that?" he asked as she tilted her head back and forth, as if trying to dislodge the water from her ears.

"Only when I'm stressed or sexually frustrated." Sara walked closer to the steps while shaking her head. Her cheeks again pinkened, and not from her strenuous exercise. He handed her the beer he'd brought out for her, and she took a swig and scrunched her nose. Not a big beer drinker. He was figuring out all of her little quirks, studying her like she was a science project, his project.

"I have a single cure for both of your problems. Want me to show you?"

She rolled her eyes while ringing the water out of her hair.

"What happened to the arm?"

Sara fingered the bandage before waving away his concern. "It's just a scratch." She ran a hand over her face, and the smile that had once been there was replaced with a frown. "You have a unique case. Stalkers generally only target their victims, and yours is targeting your ex-girlfriends. She's eliminating anyone that she sees as a potential obstacle standing in her way of the ultimate prize." She tilted her head toward him. "In this case, that would be you, Don Juan."

His Don Juan attributes seemed to be lacking tonight, either that or she was immune to his charm and charisma.

She shrugged. "You're one hundred percent prime, Grade A steak, not to mention successful, smart, rich, and even sexy."

"You think I'm sexy?"

She ignored his question, took another sip, and made another face. "Since it goes against the classic stalking, I'm wondering if the killer just wants to make it look that way. Maybe she or he is trying to frame you."

Wait… what? Sexy…yeah, he could work with that, but she'd switched gears way too fast before he'd even had a chance to comment. He'd come down to the pool to unwind, maybe get to know Sara better. The flirting had been a bonus. Even though the murder was still fresh in his mind, he'd wanted to forget, even if for just a little bit. And she had the body that could give him just that.

Now it seemed he couldn't wrap his head around what she was suggesting. "Those are the only two options, stalker or someone wanting to frame me?"

She nodded and took another sip of her beer as she climbed out of the pool and then walked over to the chair where she'd discarded her robe. He knew she had a great body even if she didn't try to flaunt it. The black one-piece hugged her body like a second skin, giving him a glimpse of the beauty hiding beneath the suit. He lowered himself farther into the water and pressed up against the wall, reclining on the side of the pool, knowing if he got out of the water this minute even the cold air wouldn't do anything to diminish the bulge in his swim trunks.

She slid on the robe and tied the sash before sitting down in the chair and using the towel she'd brought out to cover her legs. "Unless you have a jealous lover out there that wants revenge, which you haven't told me about, I'm sticking with my gut feeling, but I'll try and keep my options open. One thing I'm almost certain of is that it started within the last month, so we're going to need to retrace your steps and figure out everywhere you've been. Anyone you can think of who acted weird, any new acquaintances? Also be thinking about anyone you've pissed off recently, male or female."

He gulped down the rest of his beer and propped his chin against his arms. She wasn't asking for a lot. She was asking for a damn miracle. He looked up. "Honey, you really expect for me to remember everyone I talked to in the last thirty days. I've been to ten fundraisers and benefits alone. I wouldn't even begin to know how to start remembering."

Sara chewed on her bottom lip before sliding out of the lounge chair to her feet. "Then we'll have to wing it."

She started walking back toward the pool house.

"Wait! What?"

Stopping at the door, Sara turned. "Make sure you lock up and get a good night's sleep. We've got a busy day tomorrow, so expect to get hot and sweaty."

She chuckled as she disappeared into the pool house, leaving him to his thoughts.

Hot and sweaty he could handle. Collin pushed off the wall and floated on his back. Yeah, that was exactly what he needed, a night off. A plan started forming in his head on exactly how he was going to win over the little investigator. Maybe a candlelight dinner, slow dancing, and conversation. She wouldn't stand a chance against his charms or the seduction playing out in his head.

# 7 CHAPTER

Collin shoveled the dog poop from the kennel into a nearby wheelbarrow. Sweat trickled down his back as the stench from the surrounding cages threatened to overwhelm him. He glanced over at the next stall. "Hot and sweaty, you're a riot."

She grinned. "Suck it up, rich boy. I warned you."

"You could have at least warned me that I'd be doing manual labor. Hell, I would have worn my old sneakers." Who was he kidding? He would have talked her out of coming here to begin with. "Why are we here again?"

Sara laughed at his unease, her voice a sweet reminder of what she'd implied. Now only if she'd just give in.

"You remember that picture they took this morning of us standing in front of the building?"

He swiped the beads of sweat from his forehead. "Yeah."

She gave him a mischievous grin. "I called in a favor and we're going to be on the front cover of the society pages in tomorrow's newspaper. I hope you don't mind."

She stopped shoveling and leaned against the handle of the shovel. She gestured to the stalls. "This is just *my* way of giving back to the community. I love animals. Don't you?"

His head snapped up, and he propped the shovel against the fence. "I could have just written them a check." He threw his hands up in the air. "Hell, I could have hired someone to come clean out all of these kennels."

She stepped out of her cage, and he watched as a beautiful dog as black as midnight came running down the hall with a purple leash flailing behind his wagging tail. The dog looked healthy and loved, like he could have belonged in a family. Not like the animals he would have expected to find in the kennel. He jumped up into Sara's arms, lapping at her face with his long pink tongue. If he had to guess, the dog was a lab and was able to make Sara smile, something that even Collin hadn't figured out how to do on a regular basis.

Sara went down to her knees, scratching the dog behind his ears. "I missed you too, Spike."

The dog's tail whipped back and forth as his pink-and-black spotted tongue continued to assault her face, leaving slobber in its path as he continued giving her puppy kisses. Sara sat the dog down and started petting the canine, and her face radiated with a joy he'd yet to witness. *Lucky dog.* He had to figure out a way to get her to smile more. "This is why I do it."

She kissed the dog's head once more and rubbed the dog's coat before she pushed to her feet. "They don't have a lot of volunteers here. Besides, I enjoy coming to see Spike."

"I can see that." Collin stepped out of his stall and pointed to the puppy. "Why don't you adopt the mangy mutt so you can see him all of the time without having to pick up a shovel?"

She ran her hand over the dog's sleek black fur on his head and around his ears. "Did you hear what that mean man called you, Spike?" She kissed him and continued to stroke down the dog's coat. "He doesn't know what he's talking about does he?"

Sara stood and patted his head one more time. "I wouldn't be able to take care of him." She sobered. "My work takes me away at a moment's notice, and I can be gone for weeks at a time."

Her shoulders sagged but only briefly before Spike jumped up at her again, as if he could sense her mood. She grinned and pulled a treat out of the smock she was wearing and fed it to him. Seemingly satisfied, Spike wagged his tale as he trotted back down the hall the way he'd come.

Collin rose, stepped up behind her, and started massaging the knots in her neck. She moaned and closed her eyes. "Sara, I know it's only part of the ruse, but I enjoy spending time with you." She stiffened under his ministrations, but he kept working at relieving her tension anyway. She'd eventually get used to him touching her, but a bigger test was coming. One that included much more than a back massage. "Don't go reading anything into it. I just think that it would be nice if we were friends. That's all."

She stepped out of his reach, and his hands fell to his sides.

"I think we're done here." Her voice cracked as she spoke.

"Done as in no way we'll be friends? Or done here as in no more shoveling and you're ready to go?"

She gave him a warm smile. "Done as in I stink and need a hot shower, so let's leave."

He grabbed both shovels, carried them out the back door, and rinsed them off before returning them to where they belonged. "It's probably good we're leaving. We still need to pack."

"Pack for what?" She reached behind her to undo the smock, but he brushed her hands aside and untied the knot for her. His fingers brushed against the soft skin of her neck as he lifted it over her head. The scent of strawberries from her shampoo drifted to his nose as he briefly leaned against her back before stepping back and removing the one he had worn. He hung them both up on the pegs.

"We have a benefit fundraiser in Quinton, Alabama for a cancer organization," he replied, pleased at how nonchalant he sounded at the thought of their first big test of being a couple, even though it was fake. "Didn't you even look at the schedule Regina gave you?"

Her brows drew together as he placed his palm on the small of her back and steered her out of the kennel. Unable to hide the amusement of watching her chew on her bottom lip, he leaned over and whispered, "Don't worry. We aren't sharing a hotel room, and we'll have a chaperone for this trip."

"Oh, honey, I'm not worried." She winked. "I am more than capable of keeping you in line, but I think with everything going on, that we need to make you less of an available target. We just need to be seen together making out and for the picture to make the papers. After that, you're services won't be required for me to do the rest."

He shook his head. Even though she was right, his showing up at the events meant more. It was his way of helping. "My schedule shouldn't matter. I'm not the killer's target." He held open the SUV door for her. "You are."

He shut the door and slid into the passenger seat.

"Yeah, but I only need one really good sexy showing to entice the stalker to want to take me out, and I can do that with my hands tied behind my back."

She revved the engine and pulled out of the drive.

"Maybe since we're going out of state the killer won't follow us. Maybe it will be a peaceful weekend and we can relax."

"And maybe pigs will fly and the killer will turn herself in. Collin, obsessed people don't stop just because you crossed the state line."

\*\*\*\*

Sara leaned back into the leather seats of the private jet, courtesy of Lexi's billionaire husband. She'd spent the rest of the evening avoiding Collin while she packed. She'd checked in with Marco, Lexi, and Catherine. Lexi had reminded her that, a few short months ago, it had been a family member actually embezzling from her fake husband. It was her best friend's words that reminded Sara that everyone needed to be considered a suspect. Sara let her gaze rove over to Regina. What did she really know about the woman? Nothing, except that Collin trusted her. Regina knew his schedule like the back of her hand. She had the information at her fingertips. Was it possible Regina wanted more from him? She made a mental note to discuss it with Collin when they reached the hotel. Until then, Sara would watch her as carefully as she would any other suspect.

Regina's glare met Sara's watchful gaze. Neither one of them spoke a word. They didn't have to. Regina was sizing Sara up just as much as she was Regina. The woman was all legs and blonde; everything that Sara wasn't. She was refined by the look of her perfectly polished outfit and pumps. Initially Sara had thought high maintenance, but now she wasn't so sure. The only thing really off about the young assistant was her eyes. Her impeccable makeup did little to cover the bags sagging beneath her young eyes. Was it from a night of partying or something more? Her eyes were glassy. From a sleepless night or crying? Sara couldn't tell. Yep, the assistant's background would require more scrutiny. Sara would uncover any skeletons in the woman's closet. It was just a matter of time.

Sara flipped open the newspaper in her lap, intent on checking to see that she and Collin had indeed made the society section. Her grip on the paper tightened. Staring at Sara was a portrait of Congressman Benton's family with a redhead smack dab in the middle. Not just any redhead, but the same redhead that had been tied up in handcuffs at the shady club with Senator Boyles a few short nights ago. Sara speed-read the article, and her hand flew to her mouth as she gasped. "Oh…." She shook her head. "This can't be happening."

Collin closed his laptop and leaned over her shoulder. "What's not happening?"

She couldn't disclose her last assignment, but she wouldn't have to. She handed him the paper. "Congressman's Benton's daughter, Natasha, was found murdered last night."

His brows dipped as he took the paper from her hand. His shoulders slumped as he read the article. Evidence that the news bothered him for a different reason than it bothered Sara. No one spoke a word as the plane landed and they got into the SUV's that were supposed to carry them to the hotel.

They rode in silence. Sara's mind was racing with questions on Natasha's disappearance and death. She needed to talk to Marco. Chances were he'd already read the papers and was aware of the connection but she needed to know what was going on.

Collin had been true to his word. They did have separate rooms, but he'd made sure that hers adjoined his, only separated by a door with a lock on it. The rooms were more like suites, each having a separate bedroom and lounge area with a television. More fancy than any place she would have chosen.

She hung her dress up in the closet and glanced down at her watch. They had several hours to kill before the benefit. A knock sounded on the door separating her room from Collin's. She unlocked it and pulled it open. Collin was lounging against the doorframe on the other side.

"I'm going across the hall to Regina's room to go over my schedule, and then we're going down to get something to eat. It's as good a time as any to start flaunting our relationship. Don't you think?"

"How about you come get me when you're ready to go eat? I need to check in with Marco and take care of a few things."

\*\*\*\*

"Oh my god…it's you! It's you!"

For the third time that evening, Sara leaned back in her chair in the swanky five-star hotel restaurant and watched as Collin smiled adoringly at the flocks of young teens surrounding the table. Sara bit her lip to resist mocking the women. The low lighting, meant to give off a romantic mood, made it difficult for her to watch their movements as they pulled out markers and magazines with Collin's picture plastered on the cover, all wanting autographs and photos. Some wanted his signature written on what little breasts had formed, as if they were at a heavy metal concert.

Sara leaned into Collin. "Don't even think about it. Child molestation is a crime in this state."

Collin choked on his water and cleared his throat.

The flashes of the camera bulbs were almost blinding. Somehow all of Alabama had figured out where they were staying, and that wasn't going to be good for security or keeping horny women under control. Collin was what she called a triple threat: sexy as sin, undeniably rich, and from what she could tell…a decent guy on top of it all. She couldn't imagine a single woman on this earth that would turn him away if he pursued her. As it stood, he had it all and his title as the world's most eligible bachelor added a bit of glam to his already glamorous life. Who wouldn't want to be rubbing elbows with the hottest guy in the universe?

Regina leaned over and patted her hand. "You'll get used to it."

"Not in this lifetime." Sara would never get used to sharing her date with the entire female population, and some of these women were beautiful, stunning even. Sara shook her head. Dealing with it for a few weeks was plenty, and if this was any taste of things yet to come, she really needed to step up her game and find the killer. Sara let her gaze rove over the rest of the restaurant. She stopped on a woman wearing a hoodie and jeans standing just outside the shadows with her head down. The hoodie was effectively blocking her face; a few of her blonde strands poked from beneath the hood. Shy, maybe; suspicious, definitely. Sara placed her napkin on her plate and rose. "Excuse me."

She went to move around the table, never taking her eyes off the woman standing near the exit. Collin caught her arm and she hesitated before glancing down at him. His questioning gaze held hers. She looked back toward where the woman once stood to find that she'd vanished.

Her eyes scanned the restaurant and she never spotted her again. She sat back down. Tension filled her shoulders as an unease settled in her gut. She leaned into Collin and whispered, "You're a sitting duck. We need to move."

The waiter appeared, and Collin signed the bill and stood. He slipped his fingers through hers and kissed her cheek. More cameras flashed, taking pictures as Collin and Sara walked hand in hand and stepped onto the elevator, followed by Regina. With the door closed, Sara pulled her Glock out of her ankle holster. The tension in the elevator was thick. Everyone was silent as they watched the red numbers moving up until the elevator dinged the arrival to their floor. Sara poked her head out, making sure the hall was clear before she motioned for them to move. She slid her card key in the slot, pushed the door open, and pulled Collin inside.

"Don't you think the gun is a little much?"

"No."

"They just wanted my autographs and pictures. It happens everywhere I go."

"It sucks to be you." Sara checked the bathroom. "One of them could've been your stalker."

He stood unmoving with his arms pegged against his chest. A move she'd only ever seen him do when he got defensive, which didn't happen often. "I'm not going to be scared into hiding. I have obligations to fulfill."

His voice held a hint of annoyance. No, not annoyance, anger. Laying her gun on the night stand, she sat down on her bed. "Are they worth risking your life?" She glanced up. "Because that's what you're doing. I can't protect you during all of these appearances and impromptu fan mobs. You're going to have to compromise."

"You don't understand." He turned his back on her.

She abruptly stood. This was a conversation they needed to have. She needed to understand what made him tick; she needed to understand what was going on in his head. "Then explain it to me," she demanded in her hardened tone without a hint of sympathy, fake or real. "You can live without being the center of attention for two weeks; it's not going to kill you, but the stalker might."

He spun around and closed the distance between them. Molten blue swirled in his eyes like an angry storm fighting to break free. He grabbed her arms. "Is that what you think? That I'm so shallow that all I care about is getting my fucking picture taken? I already told you it was for charity."

Sara pointed to the door. "You can fool yourself, Collin, but you can't fool me. Those women didn't care about how much money you're bringing to the charity; they weren't pulling out their checkbooks to write charity donations for tonight. That mob scene was unnecessary." Sara sighed with exasperation. "Explain to me why this is so important." She demanded. She balled her fist and clenched her teeth. Why in the hell didn't he understand that he was in danger... and not from the mob of women but from a god damn killer!

His hands fell to his sides, and he stepped back and again turned his back on her. "These foundations count on me. I don't know why people peg me as famous or why they're willing to pay money to get their pictures taken with me. But if money from just my presence can save one life, then it was worth it."

She stepped up behind him and placed her palms on his arms. "I'm sorry, Collin, but you're going to have to face facts. Some lunatic is willing to kill to get her hands on you."

He turned and placed his palm on her face. Acutely aware of his proximity, she noticed the lines around his mouth soften. He slowly leaned down. When he spoke next, it was against her lips. "If you're my girlfriend, they're going to expect me to kiss you."

He did a complete one-eighty right before her eyes. Nowhere in their conversation had they been discussing whether or not she could pull off acting like his girlfriend. Her eyes searched his, looking for answers to her unspoken question. She wasn't sure if she leaned in to close the gap between them or if he had. His arms came around her and pulled her close to his body as he pressed his unrelenting lips to hers. It only lasted mere seconds before he pulled back, but it was enough of a taste and a tease for her to realize she wanted more of his touch, more of his mouth. *Double damn fire.* She stepped back, shaking the crazy thoughts from her head.

"What was that for?"

He gave her a lopsided grin, not that of a confident man, but as one testing the boundaries after walking his date to the door and debating on whether to give her a good-night kiss after a first date. "Figured we needed to get that out of the way if your performance tonight is going to be believable."

She glanced down at her watch and walked to the door separating their rooms. She flicked the lock and pulled the door open. "You need a time out, and I need to start getting ready."

Stepping into his room, Sara checked every nook and cranny before she deemed it safe for him to enter. She walked to the door and flicked the extra latch on the door to ensure he was secure and safe for the time being. "I'll feel better if we keep the door open until we leave."

Resting his palm on her shoulder, he leaned over and kissed her cheek before disappearing into his room. *Rein it in, Sara. Now is not the time.* She checked herself against familiar lust brewing inside of her; the heat searing down-to-your-bones kind that only he seemed to have figured out how to trigger from her. Damn, just what the hell had she gotten herself into? She went back to her room, all the while listening to the news he was watching on the television next door. She heard him puttering around even as she went about getting ready.

She stepped into the floor-length black silk dress, laced her arms through the spaghetti straps, and zipped it as far as she could reach, leaving her back half exposed. She struggled to pull up the damn zipper, struggling for just the right angle, only stopping when the muscle in her arm cramped. She knocked on the open door to Collin's room before walking in. Seeing him in his tighty-whities was the last thing she needed. She envisioned that picture and amended that he was probably a boxer guy. He was lounging against the headboard, already dressed in his tuxedo pants. His jacket hung off a nearby chair, and his crisp white shirt hung buttoned but un-tucked.

"Damn, I guess I'll never know."

He quirked a brow. "Know what?"

"Boxers or briefs."

He chuckled as he slid off the bed. "There's still time for you to find out."

She turned, showing him her back. "Do you mind?"

Over her shoulder, she watched as his eyes seemed to undress her and delivered a nonverbal invitation in the smoldering depths. It would be way too easy to get lost in the way he looked at her. Her breath hitched when his fingers touched her bare flesh, sending shivers down her spine. What should have been a simple soft touch could have turned into so much more if she'd relented and given in. The small of her back was a small void untouched in what seems like years. His touch was almost enough for her to throw caution to the wind and turn into his hands, wanting a more intimate caress.

She glanced over her shoulder. "And that's not an invitation, Romeo. The direction is north."

His fingers brushed her skin, and they moved down to grasp the zipper, giving it a slow, agonizing tug into place. Pure torture and the sad part was that she'd asked for it.

His palms moved to caress her arms. His hot breath brushed the crook of her shoulder up to her neck. His voice was low and purposefully seductive as he whispered into her ear. "You're beautiful."

She turned in his arms, trying desperately to keep her composure. His body was mere inches from hers. Her body stirred, hyper aware of how close he was. A heated silence between them grew as she stood in place unable to move, not that she would have, not that she could have. She drew in a deep breath. "No, no, no, Romeo. Keep your hormones in check. Little Collin can't come out to play.

"He's anything but little, baby."

Her gaze landed on his full, kissable lips before moving the short distance to his eyes. Her throat constricted as she broke through the trance he held on her. "We're going to be late."

She recognized his momentary hesitation before he dropped his hands to his sides.

She waited as he tucked in his shirt, wishing it were her hands she was shoving down the front of his pants. For research's sake, she tried to tell herself she needed the answer to her underwear question. He grabbed his tuxedo jacket and slid it on as she left the room. He waited for her while she grabbed her clutch with the gun stuffed inside. It was going to be one hell of a long night.

Her black sheath dress had no give for hiding a gun underneath. Hell, it barely left her any room to breathe, and the seams were stretched so tight there was no way in hell she'd be bending over tonight. She was forced to carry her gun the old-fashioned way and hope that would be enough to keep him alive.

# 8 CHAPTER

Sara ran through the current list of suspicious people she wanted to question as they rode the elevator down to the lobby. Regina and Drew topped the list. She knew so little about each of them, and they did have direct access to not only his house but to Collin. She needed to rule them out before anyone else. She also had yet to meet Collin's publicist, Maureen, as well as the blogger guy and the ex-girlfriend squirreled away. Maybe his exe had noticed someone unusual lurking around since she'd bumped into Collin. One could hope, even if she was grasping at straws. Her list of persons-of-interest was endless. It could have been any one of the female population or gay male population for that matter. Or, crap, even a man holding a grudge. Her mind spun from the endless possibilities, but her gut instinct was a stalker, someone who had an unhealthy fixation on him. Collin was, after all, sex on stick.

"Tell me why Regina isn't coming down with us. She came all this way, so I would assume she'd want to enjoy the party."

Collin placed his hand on Sara's back. "She doesn't like all the cameras."

They stepped into the ballroom and were immediately bombarded by flashing lights. Sara tried to smile through the pandemonium, even though her nerves were strung tight. It would be hard to catch a killer if she couldn't freakin' see. Collin steered her, through the hordes of reporters, with his hand on the small of her lower back. Reporters continued to yell questions at them, to them, about them, wanting to know who she was and how long they'd been dating.

When the black dots cleared from Sara's vision, she searched the surrounding sea of faces for threats. She cleared the area the way a cougar on the prowl looks for new prey, and she wasn't referring to the animal. Every woman and man that came close to them was in her radar. She tightened the hold on her clutch. Large open spaces and unknown people had her heart racing. Collin pulled her into his arms and kissed her cheek.

"You've got to relax, Sara. You're not very convincing as a woman in love. I thought that was what we were going for."

She ignored the chandeliers and twinkling lights, completely blocking out the conversation and clinking of glasses around her as she slid her free palm up the lapel of his jacket and around his neck.

Pulling him closer, she whispered what she'd been trying to block from her mind, "My money is on boxers."

She crushed her lips to his, eating him up and paying him back for how he made her feel. Turnabout was fair play, and it was damn sure his turn. His arms around her tightened, drawing her chest flush against his. She parted her mouth and ran the tip of her tongue along the seam of his lips. His lips parted, and that was the only invitation she needed. Her tongue dueled with his in a sensual kiss dominating and demanding, giving any onlookers a good show. There wouldn't be any question as to whether she wanted this man, no matter the circumstances, because she damn sure did. His palms caressed her back even as he tilted his head, deepening the kiss. He moaned deep in his chest as she nipped his lips once more and pulled back. "I'm right, aren't I? You're a boxer guy?

His eyes were glazed, and his lips held a tint of her lipstick. She reached up and rubbed her finger over the stain, removing any trace of their heated embrace. He captured her hand and placed a gentle kiss on her fingertip. His usually confident voice was strained with the same desire she was feeling. "Why don't we go back to the room and you can find out?"

He leaned in again, but the sound of someone clearing their throat made him pause before he'd made contact, completely ruining his chance to make good on his statement. He straightened and tugged at the bottom of his coat. His other hand tightened around her hip, pulling her closer to his side.

"Sanchez, what are you doing here?" Collin asked in a thick voice.

"I didn't believe the papers were true. I couldn't believe you'd stoop to such a new low." The portly man with the receding hairline set his gaze on Sara, and then he ran his gaze the length of her dress and back up.

"Eyes up here, buddy."

The redhead on his arm looked vaguely familiar, but Sara couldn't place her. "I had to see for my own eyes."

"See what?"

"That you would actually put another woman in danger after both of those deaths. Awfully brave of you." He glanced at Sara inquisitively, as if trying to figure her out. "And not very smart of you, sweetheart."

She immediately remembered the name. The internet blogger who'd done the exposé and put those women in danger. She held out her hand and stepped out of Collin's hold and closer to the blogger. "Actually Mr. Sanchez, it's because of you that Collin's in this predicament." She let her gaze run down his body and back up, as he'd done to her. "Let me guess...you're gay and want him all for yourself."

It wasn't until the redhead popped her pink gum that Sara remembered where she knew her from and why she looked so different. It was Little Ms. Ray of Sunshine, the sheriff's daughter that had attached herself to Sanchez's arm. No longer brunette, or blonde, now she was trying her hand at being a redhead. Remembering the Sheriff's comment, Sara surmised that the wind must be blowing outside. *Perfect match*. She silently thought to herself.

Marvin Sanchez lifted a brow above his beady eyes and smirked as he untangled the woman's hand from around his arm and clasped Sara's hand with both of his. "I'm definitely not gay, honey." He stepped closer into her space. "And I don't know how you can blame the deaths on me."

"It was your exposé that put a face and name to each of those women from his past, exposing them as targets." Sara squeezed his hand, crushing the jerk's fingers in her grip. "If it weren't for you, they might still be alive, but I'm going to tell you how you can make this right."

Sanchez chuckled. "And how's that, sugar? You going to threaten to take down my blog, print a retraction? All I did was report the truth, and anyone with half a brain could have found the information themselves."

Sara's grin grew wider. "Mr. Sanchez, when you start digging a little deeper into who I really am, which we both know you will, you'll figure out that not only am I capable of removing the list for you, but with one phone call and a few clicks, I can make it seem as though you never existed. Now let's be friends." She patted his face. "I want you to plaster pictures of the two of us together on your website. I want the whole world to see how much we're in love."

He jerked his hand away from hers. "Who the hell are you?"

She blew him a kiss and winked. "Crossed, I'm your worst nightmare, *sugar,* but if you cooperate, then maybe we'll give you an exclusive."

Okay, so maybe she was bluffing a little bit about erasing his identity, but she damn sure knew the type of people that could and would do that for her, with no questions asked. She'd met all types of people while working for the FBI, most of them agents, some that ran on the other side of the tracks, but what Mr. Sanchez didn't know wouldn't hurt him. She gave him the ultimate disrespect and turned her back on him, and then she stepped up to Collin. "I'm thirsty and bored, baby. Wanna mingle?"

Collin glanced over her head before meeting her gaze. He slid her hand into the crook of his arm and steered her away. When they reached the bar, he ordered himself a beer and she ordered a martini. What she really needed was a shot, a strong one. She wouldn't be drinking alcohol, but she could make sure that she looked the part.

Collin leaned against the bar and turned to her while they waited. "That was pretty brave of you, *sugar.*"

Sara glanced across the room to find Sanchez still staring at her and, from his expression, he was still trying to figure out just who the hell she was. She'd left him intrigued, just as she'd planned. "What's the story between you two?"

Collin took a sip of the beer placed, on the counter, in front of him. "Believe it or not, he was the football jock in school and I was the nerd but there isn't any animosity between us. I think he likes the limelight and he's using me as a stepping stone and, to be honest, I didn't mind until he did the expose on my exes."

Her eyes widened in disbelief as she turned back to him. There wasn't much that could shock Sara, but his confession sure did. "Not the other way around?" She gestured to his muscular body and sexy-as-sin good looks. "You haven't always been the stud the magazines claimed?"

He chuckled. "Hardly."

He entwined their fingers and moved her through the room to an empty table around the dance floor. "I was a computer geek. Most of my high school life was spent in front of the computer. I earned my first million before I even graduated college. The looks and body didn't come until later."

"Why were you all of a sudden worried about your looks? Not getting enough action?"

"Nah, nothing like that; it was never about my ego. My older brother joined the military and came home from Afghanistan with an injured leg. I helped him get better. I started working out with him in an attempt to push him harder and the rest, as they say, is history."

Her mouth parted in surprise and she snapped it closed. For once she kept the snappy retort to herself. Miracles did happen every day.

"Now you understand why I've got this inner need to help people and do the right thing."

"You're gay, aren't you?" She waved her hand to encompass his body. "Because there's no way you're the total package without a flaw. It's not Christmas, and I haven't been that good." What she'd read over the last couple of years, in the papers and magazines, had painted him in a completely different light, of a man oozing confidence and wealth, which weren't even Collin's best qualities. He was caring and considerate and, even though at times a bit opinionated, she liked this side of him, a side that he kept to himself and away from the rest of the world. A glimpse was all she needed to see that she'd misjudged him. She'd erroneously lumped him into the same category of other men she'd dated in the past.

"I've got baggage, sweetheart. What do you call a psychotic killer with a hard-on for my exes?"

She playfully batted his shoulder. "Oh right…there is always that."

He leaned toward her, placing his lips next to her ear. "You're like a mystery, Ms. Johnson. A puzzle I'm dying to solve."

She turned her head, her lips only inches from his. "When this is all over, I'll let you see how well you can fit the pieces together."

"It's a date." His palm slid behind her neck as he closed the distance between them. His kiss was light and hinted at promises yet to come. He rubbed circles, with his thumb, against the nape of her neck. His calloused fingers sent a fever coursing through her along with an image of him touching her elsewhere with the same finesse. He coaxed her lips open. She toyed with his tongue and savored his taste as their tongues mingled and she explored the recesses of his mouth. Passion surged through her as he tightened his grasp, holding her where he wanted her, almost as if afraid she'd vanish if he let her go.

Another person clearing their throat had him breaking the kiss, but he held her for what seemed like seconds as his eyes peered into hers, like he was trying to solve the mystery he spoke of earlier.

"Uh hum." The person cleared their throat again.

Collin leaned back, and that was when Sara caught the first glimpse of the pretty blonde standing next to his chair.

"When I told you to hire someone to protect you, I thought you'd be smart enough to bring him with you. Instead, you're here on a date?"

The blonde crossed her arms over her chest and narrowed her eyes. Whoever this woman was, one thing was obvious. She wasn't happy, and she was getting on Sara's last nerve.

Sara tightened her hold on her clutch as she tried to deduce whether this woman was a threat.

"Maureen." Collin's gaze darkened and his tone deepened. "I'd like you to meet Sara Johnson from Carrington-Hill."

Collin gestured toward Maureen. "Sara, this is Maureen Evans, my opinionated publicist."

Maureen pursed her lips and narrowed her eyes at Collin before quickly veiling her features. Had Sara not been watching the woman, she would have missed it. Well now, this was interesting. What exactly had transpired between Collin and his publicist that would garner such a look of disgust?

Sara stood and held out her hand. "It's nice to meet you. I've been assigned to work on Collin's case."

The publicist raised her brow but still shook Sara's hand. "Is that what it's called nowadays?" She turned toward Collin and pointed to her bottom lip. "You've got some red…right there."

Sara clenched her fingers together. "You need to tread lightly, Ms. Evans. I'm much meaner than I look, and I've got a right hook that will land you flat on your bony ass."

"It's obvious you can't keep your hands off him, and it's affecting your performance. I mean, look how easy it was for me to walk up on both of you, catching you unaware. What if I'd been the killer?"

"Maureen, lower your voice," Collin said, in a threatening tone, as he looked around at the nearby tables. What was he worried someone might overhear?

Her gaze was unrelenting and seemingly unforgiving. "What! It's true."

"We aren't discussing this here."

A sudden icy contempt flashed in Maureen's eyes. "Fine, we'll do this on the patio. Because make no mistake…" She gave Sara a disgusted look. "… we *are* discussing this." The blonde stomped off, her heels clicking as she marched toward the double doors that led outside.

Collin gently squeezed Sara's elbow. "You'll have to forgive her. She isn't normally like this."

Sara grinned. "I tend to bring out the best in everyone."

"I'll be right back."

She stopped him with the touch of her hand, not liking the possibilities of what could happen to him out in the open, unprotected, and with a woman with so much fire and venom she was ripe to strike. What if this chick was the stalker? Would she attempt to take him out in such a public forum, or would she wait until they were alone? Would the stalker even care one way or the other? "This isn't a good idea."

Running his palms up and down her arm, he pressed a light kiss on her forehead. "I'll be just outside the door." He glanced over his shoulder before meeting Sara's eyes. "You'll be able to see me from the table. Besides, I'm sure you're a great shot."

She watched him amble toward the doors where Maureen was impatiently waiting and tapping her foot.

"I see you've met, Maureen," Sanchez said from behind her with his hand on the back of Sara's chair.

Sara tried to ignore the man, but something told her that he wasn't going away.

"Bet you didn't know they were an item before she signed him on as a client." Sanchez shrugged. "Rumor has it she's still in love with him and, from the looks of it, she isn't too fond of you."

"Huh." Sara mulled that information around in her brain, letting the new information simmer like a pot on the stove. "I don't care if she likes me. What I want to know is why she wasn't in your exposé."

Sanchez leaned down, close enough that she could smell the alcohol on his breath. "Where do you think I got the list of names from? You're playing with fire, honey, and I'd hate to see a pretty little thing like you get burned. You might want to consider cutting your losses while you still can."

The blogger left without saying another word. He'd done enough damage just by planting a seed of doubt in her mind. A ping of jealousy settled in her gut. Stalkers, a pissed off publicist and now her own jealousies….the bachelor seemed to bring out the best in every woman around him. Oh no, no, no…this wasn't good. She pushed the useless feeling away. Sara's eyes never strayed from where Collin stood just outside the glass doorway. His arms were crossed over his chest even as Maureen spoke, emphasizing her words with wild hand gestures. The discussion was heated. Maureen paused and placed her fists on her hips. Collin reached for her, placing a palm on her arm, but she just as quickly shrugged it off. She pointed toward where Sara was sitting and Sara watched as Maureen's face turned an unnatural shade of red before she spun on her heel and stomped off, leaving Collin standing there alone. Collin ran his hand over his neck as he stood there shaking his head, still looking in the direction Maureen had departed.

He returned to their table moments later.

"She's a special kind of crazy with a shot of espresso, isn't she?"

He slid into the seat next to her. "She's a bit intense and worried. That's the only way she knows how to be."

Intense, crazy, jealous, maybe even crazy jealous. The classic definition of a stalker flashed in Sara's mind. She noted the worried look in his eye as he continued to stare at the door where they'd had their argument. "Want to talk about it?"

"She doesn't approve."

Sara leaned back in her chair and studied Collin's profile. The fine lines on his face deepened. His shoulders sagged. "Clearly. She's right, you know. I shouldn't have kissed you. I lost focus, and that isn't a good thing in my line of work, especially without backup."

He turned at Sara's admission. The lines on his face softened. "You didn't kiss me, Sara. I kissed you, and you didn't have a choice."

Collin's words were spoken with confidence and held a hint of truth. She believed he meant what he said, regardless if it meant that her kissing him back could have put him in danger. "It would be good for you to remember that I don't do anything that I don't want to do."

The orchestra started playing a slow melody, and Sara watched as people around them strolled to the dance floor. Her gaze still scanned their surroundings, searching for any sign of an impending attack or any other jealous women with fangs and claws.

Collin stood and held out his hand. "You'll have a better view from the dance floor."

She placed her fingers in his, and they moved to the center of the dance floor. His arms circled her waist and pulled her close, and he started swaying to the music. Sara tried to digest and compartmentalize everything Sanchez had implied with what she'd seen with her own eyes. The clean scent of Collin's aftershave drifted to her nose. The hard planes of his chest pressed lightly against her breasts. Every nerve ending was standing at attention. It was obvious there was things he wasn't telling her. Things that even the blogger knew about. She needed to press Collin and find out what other bits of information he might be withholding, but she wouldn't do it here. She needed a secure private location so she could grill him. The music ended, and the swaying stopped, but he didn't release her. She glanced up.

"Can we go? Have you fulfilled your obligations?"

"Not yet. I still need to do a photo shoot with some of the guests."

She nodded. The rest of the night she followed dutifully along, trying her best to keep an eye on the crowd and Collin. She glanced over to where Sanchez was standing. A cocky smile tilted on his lips as he raised a drink in mock salute to her. They'd made a banner, with the charity logo printed on it, for Collin to stand in front of to have his pictures taken with various fans. The women that slid up next to him were obvious about their intentions. Sara took a seat at a table next to the prop. She watched as woman after woman kissed his cheek, some even being bold enough to hand him little slips of paper. Every man around him respected him, and woman were enamored by his easy good looks and charming appeal. He took his sexuality to a whole new level she'd never witnessed by anyone before. This man was a charmer, a seducer, and already a pain in her ass.

Sara was so mesmerized watching Collin work the crowd that she didn't pay attention to the heavy-set gentleman that sat beside her at the table until she heard him order an Absolute Stress from a passing waiter. She'd only ever known one other person that liked that mix of alcohol.

She turned and her mouth parted, but no words came out. Senator Boyles flipped open a copy of the newspaper where she'd made the front page in her god-awful plaid schoolgirl miniskirt. He leaned in closer to her. "Ms. Johnson, I believe you have something I want."

This couldn't be happening, not while she was on assignment. Sara cleared her throat and pasted a smile on her lips. "I'm not sure what you're referring to, Senator, unless you're talking about my vote." She leaned farther into him. "It will be a cold day in hell before you ever get that."

The waiter returned with the alcohol concoction and handed it to him. Sara glanced over her shoulder and noticed two men in black, just like the ones who had been following the congressmen the other day. The security guards moved closer, now standing behind them; both of their faces were expressionless.

"Ms. Johnson, don't play games with me," the senator sneered in her ear.

Sara leaned back in her chair. "Senator, I assure you this isn't a game, and if it was, I believe I've got the better hand. Can you say the same thing?"

Collin appeared on the other side of the table and held out his hand to her. "Are you ready to go?"

If Collin noticed the tension at the table, he didn't say anything. She slipped her hand in his. "If you'll excuse me, gentlemen, I think our business here is done."

She sashayed to the elevators without a backward glance. They stepped in, and Collin waited for the doors to close before pulling her into his arms. "Who was that?"

"Senator Boyles. Let's just say, my last mission sent me to take some compromising photos of him."

His hold on her tightened. "And I take it you succeeded."

"Yeah, but I'm not sure how the senator found out. It's not like he was paying attention that night."

"I'll bet he wasn't. I'm sorry it wasn't as interesting with me. I'm sure you were bored tonight after the kind of cases you cover."

Sara gave a light push on his chest and stepped out of his embrace. "I have to admit, it was quite an eye opener watching you spin your magic, not to mention meeting Sanchez, but the topping on the cake was watching Maureen throw her tantrum."

His brows furrowed when she moved to the other side of the elevator. The space was too small, not allowing her to put more distance between them. "Did I do something wrong?"

"Depends."

# 9 CHAPTER

Her shoulders were tense when they arrived back at her adjoining hotel room. She was intent on asking him some pretty invasive questions, and she wasn't sure she actually wanted to know the answers. While he shrugged off his jacket and hung it on the back of a chair and loosened his tie, she sent a quick text to Marco about the situation with the senator and mentioned the newspaper article. By the time she was done, she turned to find Collin resting against the headboard, with his fingers laced behind his head.

"So, what's on your mind?"

Sara kicked off her shoes and moved toward the only mirror in the room. She started pulling out the hidden bobby pins holding her hair in place. As casually as she could manage, she said, "Tell me about Maureen."

She glanced at his reflection in the mirror; he was frowning as he met her gaze. "What do you want to know?"

She went back to the task of pulling pins. "How come you didn't tell me you two were an item once?" She turned to him. "Didn't you think it might be important?"

He rose from the bed and stepped over to her. He slid his fingers through her strands, simultaneously massaging her head while searching for a stray pin she might have missed. He pulled one out and held it up. "Why, are you jealous?"

Sara rolled her eyes as she side-stepped him and moved back to her suitcase to put the bobby pins away. "Hardly. The woman is a loon, but seriously, she could be another victim or worse…" Sara turned and crossed her arms over her chest. "A cold blooded killer."

"Who told you?" he asked with curiosity.

She shrugged. "Does it matter? The problem here isn't who told me, but why you didn't. I can't keep you safe if you're going to withhold information."

He stalked toward her and placed a palm on her cheek. "This was exactly why I didn't tell you. You're barking up the wrong tree. No one knows about Maureen, so she isn't in any danger, and she damn sure isn't the stalker."

His vehement refusal to acknowledge the truth momentarily angered her. Slapping him upside the back of the head came to mind. Locking him up and away from the woman population was another alternative that ran through her thoughts. She bit back her retort and tried another angle. Sara covered the back of his hand. Sensitive, she reminded herself. Collin was a good guy, and just because he was a little naïve when it came to women didn't mean he deserved her lecture.

"She's a piranha." Well, there went her idea of sensitive. "I've seen woman who will go to any lengths to win back a man. Even if Maureen isn't the stalker, she still wants you, and you're putting her in danger. I can name at least one person who knows about the history you have with her and I'm pretty pissed that it wasn't me. "

"I was going to tell you, but I know deep down that it isn't her. She's stubborn. She won't go into hiding, and she understands what is going on. That's why she was yelling at me. She wants me to get more security." He leaned down, and his lips hovered in front of hers. "Can we talk about something else?" He grinned. "Or maybe even not talk at all?"

He crushed his lips to hers and slid his palm around to the nape of her neck. A delightful shiver of want coursed through her body, touching places left dormant way too long. His body pressed up against hers, chest to chest. His bulge strained against his dress pants and pressed against her belly. His tongue tangled with hers. This kiss was slow, it was sensual, and she wanted it. A pulsing knot of need within her demanded she take more, and yet she wasn't about to let it get that far. He must have thought the kiss would end the argument; he'd thought wrong. She leaned back.

"Sara…"

"You've got to stop doing that."

"You've got to stop fighting it. What happened to the woman who wanted to know boxers or briefs? Where did she go?"

She stepped back. "She grew a brain. I'm here to do a job, nothing more."

He reached for her, stopping her retreat. "Can't you do both? This thing between us isn't going to go away. It's just going to grow and fester until it explodes. Why are you denying us the chance?"

Sara stood unable to move. His words touched a place in her heart that she'd thought was long dead. Should she? Shouldn't she? She wanted too; damn did she want pretend there was no killer. That he was actually interested in her and not just because she knew how to shoot a gun. Damn it. She placed her hand on his smooth face and held his gaze before she spoke the words she didn't want to say, something to make him understand, something to put the much-needed distance back between them, the way it should be.

"Collin, you're my assignment, and I think it's best if we keep it that way."

Annoyance and determination flashed in his eyes. The unwelcome tension stretched even tighter between them, almost to the point that it would smother them both. He quickly masked the determined look with one of annoyance. He wasn't going to drop it; she could read it on his face. This man was determined if nothing else, and she knew it was just a matter of time before she would succumb to his charms. The chemistry between them was too powerful. Tangible like a ball of rubber bands, each strand holding the others back. If one restraint were to break, the rest would explode into a whirlwind of energy, supplying them both with a sexual desire she wouldn't be able to avoid. No, she couldn't take the risk of letting herself succumb to his easy charm and sexy-as-hell looks. Her heart wouldn't withstand the trampling she knew would follow, and it was inevitable that he would eventually move on. If he could keep secrets from her, she wouldn't, and couldn't, risk the chance of having more of an emotional tie with him.

He grabbed his jacket and slung it over his shoulder. "I see. Well then, I guess this is good night."

His words were strained. Her stomach churned with anxiety. Her nerves loaded with frustration. But there was one more thing left she needed to do. She walked across the room to the other adjoining door, flicked the lock, and pulled the door open. "Sorry, Romeo, but you're sleeping in this room."

Hitching his thumb over his shoulder, he asked. "Not in my room and not yours? Now you want me to switch rooms? We aren't even registered for that room."

Bypassing him, she moved into the empty room. "You're not registered for this room, but Marco reserved it and paid for it in his name as a backup. It's better this way, just an extra security measure."

Collin leaned his head back and briefly squeezed his eyes close. "Where are you sleeping?"

"I'll be going back and forth between your old room and mine and making plenty of noise so people will assume you're in there. Maybe I'll even leave the television cranked up a notch or two.

He moved back through her room into his old one and shoved things into his suitcase, and then he wheeled it back through her room on his way to the new one. "Don't you think it would be safer if you stayed in the other room with me?"

"Safer from stalkers, yes, but not from you…I think I'll take my chances with the stalker."

He splayed a sexy grin on his face and covered his heart with his palm as if she'd stabbed him in the chest. "I'm crushed." He winked. "I *can* behave myself."

"Cut the theatrics and don't open that front door for anyone, understood?"

She noticed the moment of resignation when he realized he wouldn't be getting his way. His smile fell as he gave a slight nod. "As you wish."

His gaze caressed her face. His brows drew down in contention before he shook his head and walked into the new room she'd assigned him. He left her alone for the time being. Because really whom was she kidding? He wasn't anywhere done trying to seduce her. She'd only issued a mandatory breather and she'd fight the attraction and hold out as long as she could. She gave herself a mental slap on the back for not jumping him the minute they'd walked through the door.

She closed the door between them, grabbed her toiletries and pajamas, and walked into Collin's old room and into the bathroom. She still had to make it appear as though someone was in his room. The walls were thin. She could hear the television coming from the next room. It was muffled by the wall, sounding like a low murmur, and she was unable to make out the words. She turned on the shower and adjusted the water before fumbling with the zipper on her dress, reaching in an awkward position to grab the darn clasp. She tugged until it was loose enough for her to shimmy out of the long gown. She stepped into the shower, enjoying the hot water as it caressed her body. She washed and conditioned her hair and scrubbed the makeup from her face. Her body heated, remembering the desire in Collin's eyes, his teasing touches, and the scorching kiss. She adjusted the water temperature cooler to douse the fire that threated her sanity. Her relief was short-lived.

"I know you still want me as much as I want you," A woman's voice said from the other side of the shower curtain.

Sara felt her face flush, even though she stood under freezing water. She turned the shower off, deciding how to handle the piranha. The determined woman hadn't been in the room when Sara first entered. Crap, Crap Crap. She cursed herself for not having her gun in reach. She'd left the damn thing in the other room, like a complete rookie. Sara drew the curtain back, making sure that her body was still slightly covered. Maureen's face flushed with embarrassment before she let out a gasp and quickly tried to cover her naked body with her hands. Her lingerie was splayed on the bathroom tiles. They both stood in uncomfortable silence as Sara reached for a towel and pulled it back behind the curtain.

"Collin's not here. Did you need me for something?" Sara tried to make her voice sound understanding, but it came out laced with pity.

Maureen scuttled around in the bathroom and slammed the door as Sara stepped out of the tub and threw on her nightclothes. She pulled the door open to find Maureen already dressed again. Her demeanor had moved well beyond embarrassed straight to pissed-off. She placed her hands on her hips and stared down her nose at Sara. "I knew you were a hussy the first time I laid eyes on you. I don't know why he can't see that you're just using him for his money."

Sara chuckled. It probably wasn't the right thing to do, but she couldn't help herself. "Honey, if I was using him, it wouldn't be for his money. Have you checked out his body? I bet he knows exactly how to make a woman scream from pleasure with just one touch."

Okay, so maybe baiting Maureen was wrong, but damn, it was overdue after how rude the publicist had been. Sara tried her best for a straight face and cleared her throat. "I wouldn't know, but from what I understand, you have first-hand knowledge. Care to give me some pointers?"

Sara moved across the room to the adjoining door and leaned against it. She wouldn't let herself get into a situation with no way to escape. Maureen smirked as she turned in place, following Sara's movement. "Who told you?"

Shrugging, Sara replied, "Doesn't matter. What does matter is why you sold off the list of names to Sanchez." Sara stepped closer, unable to control the anger bubbling inside on what that list of names presented. Each one a potential life to snuff out by the deranged lunatic and this stupid bitch didn't have a clue. "You do realize your old relationship with him either makes you a suspect or a target in my eyes. So tell me, Maureen, do you want him back so bad that you'd kill for him?" Sara crossed her arms over her chest; afraid she might hit the woman, and tilted her head. "Did he leave you so scorned that you're looking for revenge?"

Maureen turned her back to Sara. "You don't know what you're talking about," she said with a slight edge to her voice. "If you think I had anything to do with those murders, then he's in worse hands than I thought."

"No worse than yours. At least I know how to shoot a gun and from the looks of it, I outsmarted you…the person who is supposed to know him best."

"You bitch." Maureen spun around in a huff. Her eyelid twitched before she lunged at Sara. She saw it coming: she recognized the balled fists and hatred flaring from the woman's eyes. Sara stopped the punch directed at her face in midair, cupping Maureen's fist. She used the momentum and swung Maureen's arm behind her back and pinned her face against the wall. Sara tugged the arm higher up Maureen's back, making the woman shriek in pain.

"Maureen, I want you to listen to me and listen well. If you ever, ever come at me again like that, I'll break your fucking arm and then press charges on your sorry ass. And I'll make it my mission in life to destroy you and your reputation."

A tear of anger or pain slid down Maureen's face. Sara didn't care which, as long as the bitch got the message. Sara gave her an extra slight shove into the wall before releasing her. Sara stepped back, crossing her arms over her chest. "Now, I know love can make women do stupid things, so we're going to chalk this up to a misunderstanding. I suggest you stay out of my way and let me do my damn job."

Maureen spun around with fire in her eyes. There was no hint of embarrassment or apology staring back at Sara. Maureen stomped out of the room without another word and slammed the door behind her.

# 10 CHAPTER

Turning on the television, Sara slid into the bed in Collin's room after retrieving her gun from her purse next door. She wouldn't be caught off guard again, not after Maureen's little striptease and whatever that was with the senator and his creepy thugs. Just went to prove what she'd been saying all along. Collin Martin had the ability to throw her off her game and it was a fact she could no longer ignore. When she gets back to town, she is going to need a one on one with Marco so she could explain. Every bone in her body was exhausted. The tension in her shoulders was strung tight. Explaining what happened to Marco, much less to Collin, was going to be a bit embarrassing, but they both needed to know about the incidents. She wasn't looking forward to describing in detail how the piranha had slipped into the room, gotten the drop on her and surprised her in the shower. How Collin reacted and dealt with the news was going to be interesting to watch. The man didn't even realize Maureen was still in love with him. Figuring out just how far Maureen was willing to go was Sara's biggest task, just another missing piece of the puzzle that kept Sara from forming a whole picture of the situation. She let her thoughts lull her into a sound sleep, unable to fight the fatigue from the last few days any longer.

Sara's eyes shot open at the sound of banging coming from the door that connected Collin's room to hers.

"Sara, open up," she heard Collin shout as the banging intensified.

Sara glanced at the bedside clock. The red numbers indicated six in the morning. Sliding out of bed, she grabbed her gun, hurried to the separating door, and yanked it open, thinking that Collin was possibly in trouble. His brows dipped before he pulled her into his warm embrace. "Thank God."

Sara leaned back in his arms, speculatively eyeing his body up and down, looking for signs that he was hurt or in trouble because he damn sure better be the way he'd jolted her awake. "What is wrong with you? Are you hurt?"

Collin released her as though she were infected with the plague. "What's wrong with me! What's wrong with you!" he demanded. "I walked into your room to find the place torn to pieces, and I'd thought something happened to you."

Sara's eyes widened as she pushed past him and stood in the doorway to her hotel room. Clothes were strewn all over the bed and on the floor. She walked over to where her purse lay open in the middle of the bed and sifted through the contents. Her jewelry and money were still there. She glanced around the room, noting that none of the furniture was out of place, and that's when she noticed the calling card left behind. Her driver's license was crammed at the top of the mirror, being held in place by the frame. Written in Fire Engine Red lipstick (and she should know since it was hers) and scrawled across the mirror was the message, *You're Number 3*.

Sara threw her arms up. A war of emotions raged within her. It seemed anyone could get a damn key to Collin's and her room. The hotel manager was going to be a dead man by the time she got through with him. "What the hell is wrong with this hotel? First Maureen and now this."

She picked up the phone and dialed Marco's number.

"What do you mean first Maureen?" Collin asked with a confused look on his face. Sara hadn't wanted to tell him like this but, under the circumstances, he needed to know and he needed to hear it from her. She held up a finger as she turned back around and spoke into the phone, explaining to Marco about the room and that she wanted a forensics team pronto to dust for prints. She nodded once and hung up.

"Explain."

She grabbed him by the arm and pulled him back into the secure room where he'd slept last night. She shut the door and flicked the lock before setting her gun down on the dresser. "You might want to sit down for this."

Standing by the bed, he crossed his arms over his chest and scowled.

"Or not, suit yourself."

She proceeded to tell him what had happened, how Maureen had shown up in his room, about their confrontation, and the way things ended. By the end of the story, Collin had plopped down on the bed and had his elbows resting on his knees as he ran a hand through his hair and squeezed his neck.

He reached for the phone. "She went too far this time." He hit four buttons on the phone and waited with the receiver pressed to his ear. "I told you what would happen if you pulled another stunt like that again. I'm sorry, Maureen, but you're fired."

The rest of the conversation was drowned out. Her mind was stuck on that one word he'd said. *Again.* As if it had happened before. Not that it was her business, but she wondered if Maureen had gotten her way last time. *Again.* The woman obviously hadn't moved past whatever type of relationship they'd had. *Again.* Could her determination be chalked up to something a stalker would do, or was it merely that of a woman trying to win the heart of a man she loved? The secrets he was keeping from her were compounding. She took a deep breath and released it, but even that didn't calm her down.

Her stomach rolled, and her throat constricted as she tormented herself with *what if* scenarios. What if she'd given into Collin and slept with him in her room? What if the stalker had found them together asleep and unaware? She cringed thinking she might have gotten them both killed.

Her cell phone beeped in her hand. She glanced down at the incoming text message from Marco that assured her the forensic team was on the way and for them to stay put and not to shoot room service when it arrived. Only Marco would think that she'd be able to eat at a time like this. The thought of food wasn't high on her list of priorities. Coffee, now that was another story altogether.

There was no way in hell she was going to tell Collin about the implied threats from the senator. Threats that she had no doubt the powerful man would make good on. No, for now, that was for Marco and her to worry about. Her stomach started to settle, as she remembered that she'd hidden the memory stick and pictures the senator was after in a safe place. Just like Lexi and Catherine, she also had her own little hiding place that the others knew about if anything happened to her. With Lexi, it was her bras. With Catherine, it would be hidden in the soles of her shoes, but for Sara, it was in a secret hiding spot. Only Lexi and Catherine would know to look under the false bottom in the can of her favorite imported coffee.

**** 

"Well, that went well," Collin said as he hung up the phone. He'd always been a sucker for a woman crying, but not this time. He'd fired her, and he meant it. His heart had hammered in his chest when he walked into Sara's room to find it tossed with the message on the mirror. He'd been sick to his stomach as he pounded on the door. Every minute that had ticked by seemed like an eternity while he waited for her to answer. He almost fell to his knees when she did. He'd questioned his judgment that maybe Maureen had been right. Maybe he shouldn't have brought another woman in as a target. Marco had suggested Sara, pretending to be his girlfriend, was the best way to handle his situation, but now he wasn't so sure, doubting not only himself but her as well.

"Sara…" He turned to find her staring, lost in her own thoughts. He wanted to plead with her, hoping that maybe she'd come to her senses and decide that his case was too dangerous. "I think this was a bad idea."

She shook her head. "This is exactly what we wanted." She glanced back at the closed door. "We wanted an attack, and we got one. Now let's just hope we can stay focused, lift some prints, and catch this bitch before anyone else gets hurt."

Sara could be so aggravating at times, and it wasn't just because she'd turned down his offer to sleep with him. She was headstrong and things were getting a little too close for comfort. A knock sounded on the door before he could reply. She held up her finger and gestured for him to stay put as she moved swiftly to the door with her gun in her grip. She peeked out the peephole before shoving her gun in the back of her PJ's and pulling the door open. A man walked in, pushing a steel cart filled with covered plates. The bellboy glanced around the room but didn't say a word as he entered and scurried out just as quickly.

"Help yourself." Sara gestured toward the food. "Marco doesn't want us leaving the room, so he ordered us breakfast. For your safety, we'll be escorted back by another team."

**** 

The trip back hadn't taken long, especially since they weren't flying commercially. Sara walked into the pool house, expecting to find everything how she had left it. She'd been wrong. Someone had been able to slip by the security detail. Furniture was overturned, and the clothes from her closet were now scattered around the room. Sara pulled her weapon and moved on silent feet throughout the rest of the house. When she knew the premises were secure, she went straight to her coffee can and grimaced to find the coffee dumped on the counter and all of the food on the floor. She reached into the coffee can and removed the false bottom. She slid the pictures and the memory stick from their hiding spot and made her way back to the main house. This hadn't been done by the stalker. No, this had the senator's name and his thugs written all over it.

Sara left Collin in good hands with Lexi and Catherine and a whole team of security around his house. She informed her friends on the status of the pool house and that she needed to go see Marco. The fact the stalker had gotten so close to her at the hotel, and now an intruder had broken in while they were gone, worried her. No, it did more than that; it pissed her off. She was a damn good agent, and she hadn't heard the commotion coming from her hotel room. It should have been her going to check on Collin, but he'd come to check on her. He could have walked in while the stalker was still there and the ramifications of that shook her to the core.

Pushing Marco's door closed, Sara plopped down in one of the empty seats across from him and tossed the negatives on his desk. "Those are the negatives of the senator; you might want to keep them some place safe. I believe the senator has already been looking for them."

She explained about the vandalized pool house.

"Maybe I should pull you from Collin's detail. You're bringing more threats to his doorstep than he initially had."

Sara frowned. She hadn't really thought about it that way. But it was true, even though she wasn't ready to give up her detail. She'd never been pulled from an assignment in her whole career. "If you remove me from the case, the stalker is going to think that the reason I'm no longer around is because she ran me off. She's not going to be interested in taking me out of the equation any longer if she no longer sees me as a threat." She shrugged. "I'll just have to be more vigilant where the senator is concerned."

He sat in silence but eventually nodded. "I'll stick a team on him so we won't have any more surprises."

That eased her mind, but only somewhat. She had a feeling the senator wasn't going to stop until he got what he wanted. "Tell me the team found prints at the hotel room. Give me something to work with."

He shook his head, even as he clicked at the computer. "No prints. But we've tapped into the hotel's surveillance video." He tapped a few more times at the keys. "Come take a look and tell me what you see."

Rounding the desk, Sara stood next to Marco and watched the screen. The hall in the hotel was dimly lit, the video only partially static. Only a few people lingered by the camera, including a man and a woman dressed in a ball gown, groping each other like teenagers as they made their way into a room. Several minutes had played by when she noticed the next man. A man stopped and knocked on Regina's door. He glanced up at the camera before Regina opened the door. Sara recognized the handsome face immediately. He had the same smile and stature as Collin, and he was fidgeting as though he was nervous, glancing up and down the hall. *Drew Martin.* Regina grabbed the front of his shirt and pulled him into her room and out of sight.

*Well, that's interesting.*

She continued to scrutinize the video, every sound, every moment, anything to give them a lead. Marco didn't even ask about who'd just entered Regina's room. He must have known as well as she had who the night visitor was. Marco fast forwarded, and the time on the video now read two hours later when another figure appeared on the screen. A female with black curly hair poking out beneath a black hoodie pulled over her head. She was wearing black pants with gloves covering her small hands as she sauntered down the hall. This woman was smarter, avoiding a face shot toward the camera's lens. She grabbed the handle to Sara's room and slid in what looked like a key card, keeping her head down. Marco froze the frame and pointed an accusing finger at the figure breaking into Sara's room. "There's your stalker. What does this tell you about her?"

Sara crossed her arms over her chest as she studied the still figure. "She's smart, almost professional. Not once did she let her face be caught by the camera. Those aren't the actions of a psychotic woman. She's cool and calculating, and she's going to be harder to catch than I thought."

Marco rubbed the stubble on his face. "We assumed we were dealing with an obsessed woman with tunnel vision, one that would make mistakes, but we were wrong."

Marco clicked on the keyboard again and fast-forwarded farther into the video. The black-haired woman pulled the door silently closed so that it didn't make a sound. No wonder Sara had slept through the destruction of her room. She left via the other end of the corridor and pushed through the door to the stairwell, disappearing out of sight. After all of this, they'd come up with zilch. Marco turned in his chair as Sara retook her seat. What did she know? What had the tape proven?

"What does that video tell you?"

"We can mark Regina off the suspect list; I'd say her alibi is pretty tight."

Marco gave her a slight nod. "What else?"

"The stalker is a female who knows what the hell she's doing, although I don't think she has black hair. She's too smart to hand us that little detail on a silver platter."

Marco grinned as he leaned back in his chair. "We also know the unidentified woman had a key and, if we can find out who gave it to her, we might be able to get a description."

As much as Sara wished it was going to be that easy, she doubted it. "The key was probably stolen. I have a feeling, whoever she is, she wouldn't have made such a rookie mistake."

"I'll check the videos of the other floors to see if we can figure out what room she came out of, or where she returned to. Hopefully, we'll be able to catch her with a room number and a copy of the hotel manifest."

# 11 CHAPTER

Sara returned to Collin's house after her meeting with Marco. Her mind raced with thoughts of everything she'd learned, everything they still didn't know. Lexi and Catherine followed her out the French doors to the pool house with concern and determination in their eyes. They were her best friends. After years of working together in the FBI, they'd all bonded almost to the point of knowing what each one was thinking, and right now, if she had to guess, they were concerned. And not the *what the hell are you doing with him* kind of concern, but the deep concern that expressed, *what the hell are you going to do now and your ass better stay alive*. She was surprised to find the house cleaned and everything put back in place, except for her prized possession. The coffee was unsalvageable.

"We both pitched in and knocked it out in no time flat." Catherine said as Lexi nodded in agreement.

And that was another reason she loved her friends. She smiled. "I didn't think you two knew how to clean."

Catherine waved her hand. "Bitch, please, we've both lived on our own for a long time."

They plopped down on the couch as Sara grabbed a water bottle from the kitchen and returned moments later.

"What can we do to help you with the stalker?" Catherine's brows dipped.

If Sara knew the answer to that, she wouldn't be in this predicament. The three of them were smart, all graduating with honors. They should be able to figure out what step to take next, but right now, Sara's mind was drawing a big blank. "I have no idea. This woman moved with precision, almost as though she's been trained, or maybe this isn't her first time."

Lexi and Catherine exchanged a worried look before Catherine spoke up. "We'll look into Collin's history and check the backgrounds on all of his exes for prior arrests or restraining orders or even some type of specialized training."

That was a start. Her stomach was in knots, not because the stalker was now on to her but, because she'd let her guard down when she'd gone to sleep.

"So what's your plan?" Lexi asked.

Sara shrugged. "Collin has the next few weeks filled with meetings and not much else. The next fundraiser is at the end of the month. I think I'm going to make myself an easy target while keeping him squirrelled away. After this weekend, I think it's safe to say that the stalker has her eyes set on eliminating me from the equation." Sara grinned as a plan started to form, one the stalker wouldn't be able to resist. "Anyone up for a shopping trip?"

"Absolutely..." Catherine chimed in. "...I can always use more shoes."

Sara chuckled. "I was thinking more like lingerie. That should drive any woman jealous enough to attack again. And it wouldn't hurt having you two with me to watch my back."

"How are you going to spring the trap? You've got to send her a message, and not knowing who she is kind of makes that difficult."

Sara grinned. "Let me deal with that."

They made arrangements to meet the next day. She was going to make an event out of it: shopping for clothes, having lunch, and spending the afternoon out with her friends. After Lexi and Catherine left, she set her plans into motion. She picked up the phone and called in some favors. She glanced down at her watch and cursed. She only had an hour before her meeting.

Sara pulled up to the empty mall parking garage and parked right next to the door leading inside the three-story mall. She quickly walked to the lingerie store where her stage was set, spotting the blogger right where she'd told him to set the stage. The lingerie store lights were on. A few women lingered inside, not patrons, but the owner and another employee. Each was going to play a part in Sara's ruse. Sara grinned as she walked in the store. The manager handed her a fistful of lingerie pieces on hangers as she led the way back to the dressing room. "We're ready whenever you are."

Sara shimmied into the most respectful one. If you could call it that. It was black and sheer everywhere that didn't provide essential coverage. It was something that Sara wouldn't normally purchase, not that she'd have anyone to model it for. Her face flushed as she studied her reflection in the mirror. She stepped out of the changing room, thinking that maybe just this once her idea hadn't been thought all the way through.

The manager reached up and pulled the ponytail out of Sara's hair and gestured for Sara to follow her. They moved to the middle of the store where the manager looked out to the front of the store and nodded before she moved to pretend to be adjusting the loose straps of the camisole.

"Action," the manager said enthusiastically as if she were directing the next big box office hit. Sara couldn't help but grin.

Within seconds, Sanchez stood in the doorway with his high zoom lens in his hand. "I got it."

Sanchez let his gaze lower to her bare legs. He whistled long and low. "Damn, sugar, you're really trying to piss her off."

Sara straightened, crossing her arms over her chest. "I want it on your blog by nine in the morning, and I want you to make it a big to-do that

I'm buying new lingerie to spice up Collin's and my sex life. I also want you to mention that you just took the picture and uploaded it."

Sanchez tilted his head to the side. "You don't ask for much, do you, sugar? Why tomorrow?"

Sara spun on her bare feet. "Because she needs to know where she can find me."

"You think it's smart to call her out?"

Sara glanced over her shoulder. "I've got to get a message to her somehow and, right now, I think you're the key."

She purchased the sexy little lingerie and walked with Sanchez out to the parking garage. She pushed through the steel door and threw her hand across Sanchez's chest, effectively stopping him in his tracks. "Stay here."

She reached down, slid her gun out of her ankle holster, and dropped her bag and purse on the ground. She checked the area before moving around her car.

"Son of a bitch slashed all four tires," she said to Sanchez as she reached for her phone to call Marco. She spotted a note stuck beneath her wiper blades. "Next time, it's your throat."

She pocketed the paper and spun around with her weapon pointed in one hand and the ringing phone pressed against her ear, hyper aware of every sound and movement in the darkened shadows. She gritted her teeth as Marco's phone rolled over to voice mail.

She returned back to Sanchez. His face was pale, but he hadn't moved. "Did you drive?"

He didn't answer.

She snapped her fingers in front of his face. "Focus....did you drive?"

He nodded. She slipped the keys from his hand, grabbed him by the elbow and started walking farther into the darkened garage. "Which vehicle?"

He pointed to a four-door sedan.

She clicked the unlock button and slid into the driver's seat as he shoved his gear in the back and hopped in the passenger's side.

"What the hell was that back there?" Sanchez looked out of the back window before he turned toward her. "Does that mean the killer already knows about you?" His hand came up to cover his mouth. "And what does that mean for me?"

Sara rolled her eyes. "I'm not sure if it was the killer or not. There are a lot of people who don't particularly care for me."

"Imagine that." He mumbled beneath his breath. Sanchez crossed his arms over his chest and turned to look out the side window.

When she arrived at Collin's, the house was dark from the outside. Only the lights on the porch shined her way. Assuming he was asleep, she treaded quietly through the house, toward the kitchen, hoping to grab a drink on her way out of the back door. The kitchen was as dark as most of the rest of the house. The only light that illuminated the immediate counter space was the light from the moon shining in. She dropped her bag on the table and pulled a bottle of water out of the fridge. She kept her back to the shadow she'd noticed at the table. "What are you still doing up? I thought you'd be in bed by now."

Sara turned and leaned against the counter.

"I was coming downstairs for a drink and saw the car lights," Collin said, his voice breaking through the darkness. He stood and flicked on the light. "Was that Sanchez that dropped you off?"

She sipped her water, watching the play of emotions on his face. His brows dipped, he clenched his jaw, if she looked close enough she might just see steam rising from his head. Was that a bit of jealousy rearing its ugly head? Jealousy of the overweight balding blogger?

She held in her snicker. "I had to leave my car in the parking garage at the mall. My tires were slashed."

His face turned a deep shade of red. The steam was about to blow. She could tell that he was making great strides to keep his anger and worry contained. One day he'd figure out that crap like this happened to her just about every day. It was a way of life she'd become accustomed to.

"Do you think it was the stalker?"

She shook her head. "Nope, I think it was the senator." She shrugged. "Or at least one of his goons. Or, heck, it could have been some juvenile delinquents out looking for a good time."

His body went rigid. She wasn't about to tell him about the note in her back pocket. No, it would just worry him more. He moved to the other side of the table and picked up her bag. "Isn't it a little late for you to go shopping?"

Sara tried to choose her words carefully. She didn't need to be a rocket scientist to know Collin wasn't going to approve of what she'd done but, still, she owed him an explanation. It wasn't as though he wouldn't figure it out tomorrow when he saw it on Sanchez's website. She couldn't run the risk that he'd do anything brash, like showing up at the mall and ruining her plan.

Sara took a deep breath. "I came up with a plan."

He motioned toward the bag. "If it includes seeing you in the lingerie you bought, you can count me in."

He might not be getting an eyeful in person, but by nine a.m., he and the entire world would be getting a glimpse through the Internet. When she thought of it like that, Sara started doubting the plan she'd set in motion. Her semi-nude picture, flaws and all, would be bared for all to see, not just the stalker. "I let Sanchez snap a picture of me wearing the lingerie inside the store, so he could post in on his blog."

Collin's mouth parted as he continued to stare at her. He motioned toward the bag. "May I see?"

She nodded, and Collin reached for the bag and pulled out the black lingerie, holding the sliver of material up with the tips of his fingers. "You were in this, and you let him take your picture... to post on the freakin' Internet?" His once steady voice grew louder and much deeper. "Have you lost your mind! Are you looking for a stalker of your own...because this..." He wiggled the fabric. "...is going to draw a whole hell of a lot more attention than you want."

"I don't need your approval, Collin. If I wanted to do a damn striptease, I would."

"Like hell." He stepped toward her and stopped. He took a deep breath and let it out slowly. Sara leaned against the counter, grasping the countertop behind her. If he implied just one more time that her actions were stupid, he was going to land flat on his ass, and then Marco would be really pissed at her for assaulting the client. "I'm drawing out your stalker, and I'll have Lexi and Catherine with me when I go to the mall tomorrow. I've got everything covered."

He tossed the lingerie on the table. "I'd hardly say you've got *everything* covered."

Sara marched over to the French doors. "Grow up, Collin. It's not your body on display, and it's no worse than having a picture taken in my bikini." She yanked the French doors open and turned. "I know this will piss her off. She's going to make a mistake and come after me, and I plan on nailing the bitch to the wall. When everything is said and done, the picture comes down. It's as simple as that."

Sara left Collin standing in the kitchen, refusing to listen to any more of his tantrum. Who the hell did he think he was? It was her decision to make and there was no talking her out of it. She stomped into the pool house, threw on her bathing suit, and let out her frustrations the only way she knew how. She dove into the deep end of the pool. There was no pussyfooting around, no sticking her toes in to test that the temperature hadn't changed because whether she froze her ass off or not, she needed this workout. No, she dove in without giving it a second thought, the same way she handled most everything in her life.

Sara sank underwater. It was the only peaceful place she'd found growing up. The surrounding silence always helped her think. Once she'd thought about investing in scuba gear, just so she could stay underwater longer. Her mind replayed the shock of finding her tires slashed and the disagreement with Collin as she swam to the other side of the pool, holding herself and her breath underwater until all of the air swooshed from her lungs. She pushed up from the bottom and reached for the side of the pool, gasping in large amounts of air when she broke the surface.

Kicking off the wall, Sara started her laps, working her arms and legs until exhaustion set in. She grabbed the edge of the pool, trying to catch her breath. She felt the pair of eyes on her before she saw him. Standing just in view at the French doors, Collin leaned against the counter sipping out of a coffee mug, and he still looked angry.

Sara lifted herself out of the pool, grabbed the towel she'd laid nearby, and moved back into the pool house to change. Exhausted, she still had one last thing she needed to do before calling it a night. Hanging her wet bathing suit over the rod in the shower, she threw on a pair of jeans and a T-shirt and ran a brush through her soaked hair. She tried Marco's cell one more time and finally reached him.

He answered on the first ring. "Hill."

Sara shoved her foot into her shoe. "I had to leave the SUV in the parking garage at the mall. All four tires were slashed and the perp left me a warning about slitting my throat."

Marco grunted. "Damn, Sara, two vehicles in less than two weeks. You're really going to screw up my insurance premiums."

Sara laughed. "It comes with the job, Marco. I'm surprised you could get insurance at all."

He grunted again. "I'll take care of it. After the last hit and run, we outfitted the SUV you're driving with GPS and surveillance cameras. Maybe we'll get lucky and get a face this time."

"Huh… well, I'm glad I refrained from the make-out session in the back seat. You would have gotten an eyeful."

"Damn it, Sara…"

She giggled. "Just teasing, boss. But next time you might want to warn me because I'm not sure how much longer I'll be able to hold off the bachelor's advances."

"Sara…"

She grinned at the warning in Marco's tone. "Well, it's true."

"Consider yourself warned. Your next one will have the same gear."

She shoved the comm in her other ear. "Testing…Testing."

Dennison answered. "Go ahead Johnson."

"Just testing the equipment." She clicked the comm off.

"Are you done playing with the toys?" Marco asked with an irritated tone.

"Just seeing who you sent for security." She shoved her gun in the back of her jeans. "I want to do a sweep of the property before I hit the sack and see who else is on my team."

"What? You don't trust the new crew I sent you?"

She chuckled, "I know Dennison is capable and he can keep the others in line. Did you brief them?"

"No doll, I sent them in blind…." He sounded annoyed. "Of course, I briefed them; I'm not stupid. I needed to warn them that they'd be working with you…didn't I?"

"You're just a laugh a minute, Marco. Go get some sleep. I've got work to do." She flicked her phone closed and emerged from the pool house under the night sky. The wind rustled the leaves in the nearby trees, giving it an eerie feel. She could predict the weather from the ache in her knee. Her bones were never wrong. Rain was coming. The sound of bullfrogs croaked nearby. She inhaled a deep breath and almost choked when the heady scent of smoke drifted to her nose. She clicked her earpiece. "Who's smoking? I can smell it all the way down at the pool house."

"Negative," Five voices all responded one right after the other. Dennison was the last to chime in.

Her heart dipped into her stomach as she started jogging toward the main house. Her gaze searched the building for any sign of a fire, any sign that there was trouble. "Who's got the 20 on Collin's location?"

They all replied with their locations strategically around the property, but not one of them was inside the house. She burst through the French doors and didn't have to look far for Collin.

He was sitting back at the same kitchen table where she'd left him. His gaze shot up to meet hers as he pushed out of his chair. "Sara, what's wrong?"

"I smelled smoke." Sara turned in circles, sniffing the kitchen air. "It's not in the house."

Collin waved his hand and returned to his seat as if it was normal for someone to think that his house was on fire. "It's probably just Drew. He's one of those closet smokers that sneak out in the middle of the night on occasion to light up. He tries to hide it from me, but I've caught him on more than one occasion. He likes to go on the other side of the garden, out of sight, near the trees."

Sara relayed the message to her team and told them to check it out. She wasn't leaving Collin's side until she knew for sure there wasn't a threat in the area. Five minutes later, they confirmed Collin's guess. They indeed had found Drew with a cigarette hanging out of his mouth at the edge of the woods. Sara released a breath she didn't realize she'd been holding. "They found Drew."

He nodded. "Sara…"

Her heart hammered in her chest and didn't show signs of slowing. The thought of something happening to Collin wasn't something she was prepared to deal with and that just pissed her off more. These unfamiliar feelings needed to go back to wherever they came from. She didn't have time to deal with them, not here, not now, and she was definitely not discussing them with him. Her determination not to cave to his demands held steadfast. She didn't know what was running through his mind, but she knew where hers was headed and there was no time for that crap. An agent that falls for a client is a dead agent. Time to put some much needed distance back between them so she can do her job and not get Collin or herself killed. Sara pursed her lips together. She held up her hand. "Forget it, Collin. I'm sorry you don't agree with how I do my job, but it is the only way I know to keep us both alive. It is what it is. Good night."

With the perimeter secure to her liking and the night shift on duty, Sara dragged her exhausted body into the pool house, crawled into bed and lay awake. Her restless mind worked overtime as she tried to figure out how she was going to keep the senator's mess at bay while she dealt with Collin's stalker.

An hour later, she was still wide-awake. The shrill of her phone pulled her from her thoughts. She glanced at the caller ID and didn't recognize the number. She answered it and wished she hadn't.

A muffled voice spoke so low she couldn't tell if it was male or female. "I want what's mine."

Sara sprang up in the bed and was pulling on her jeans as she spoke. "Why don't you come get it?"

"You think you're safe behind that iron gate?" The caller's words sent a shiver down her spine, and her heart thundered in her chest. "You're not, and I left you proof."

The caller hung up. Sara hopped out of bed, slid into her sneakers, grabbed her gun and hit the front door running.

She ran through the yard, into the house, leaving the door wide open. She skidded around the banister and took the steps two at a time and skidded to a stop outside of Collin's room. She slid the door open a crack and peered into the darkness of the room before she stepped inside with her gun tight in her hand. She went to the side of the bed where Collin was fast asleep. She breathed easier watching the rise and fall of his chest. She checked the rest of the room and came up empty.

She hurried back down the stairs and out the front door to find two guards sitting on the steps outside. She marched over to them. "I want a check of the entire grounds, now!"

They jumped to their feet. One hit the comm in his ear and relayed her demands while the other charged for the front gate.

She went back inside and checked every room, looking for a possible intruder, and double-checked the windows and doors. When she was satisfied the house was clear, she moved into the kitchen and started a pot of coffee. There was no mistaking the hate she'd heard in the muffled voice. It was only a matter of time before someone made a move and, by God, she would be ready, even if it meant she had to sleep outside of Collin's door.

She'd just sat down when one of the guards entered through the French doors. "Sara, you need to come take a look at what we found."

She grabbed her gun from the table and followed the guard outside. He led her to the back of the house, where they'd originally found Drew smoking hours ago. He pointed down at the ground, and she lowered to her knees. Lying on the green grass was a bird, not just any bird, but a dead bird with his head and neck torn from his body. "Shit."

She glanced up through the forest while rising to her feet. She pointed into the greenery. "I want a schematic of this damn place. The entire place should be surrounded by a twelve foot brick wall. I want to know what the hell is back there and how the intruder got onto the property..." She turned to the guard. "And I want it done tonight."

Good thing she wasn't sleeping anyway. Her plans had just changed from lying awake in the comfort of her bed to a long night of planning. By the time morning came and she had to go shopping, she was going to be running on pure adrenaline and coffee.

# 12 CHAPTER

Sara glanced down at her watch as Garrett, Lexi, Catherine, and the same blonde that had been with Marco when they raided Collin's ex-girlfriend's house, pulled up in the drive at seven-thirty on the dot. She still didn't know the blonde's name.

"Damn, girl, you look awful," Lexi exclaimed as she walked in.

"Did the hottie keep you up all night?" Catherine asked as she followed Lexi.

Sara groaned. "No, but slashed tires and intruders on the property will tend to do that to you."

They turned around with concerns in their eyes as the blonde followed Garrett in. He pushed the door closed and slung his arm over her shoulder. "Damn, you did have a busy night."

Sara agreed but turned toward the unknown woman. "Who are you?"

The blonde glanced up at Garrett before meeting Sara's gaze. She held out her hand. "Megan Hill."

Sara's eyes widened when she spun around to find Lexi nodding. "Yep, Megan is Marco's little sister."

Sara held out her hand. "I'm so sorry. I swear, I don't know how you do it."

Megan laughed; she reached for Sara's hand and shook it. "He isn't that bad. A little over-protective growing up, but he means well."

Sara walked them into the kitchen. After a round a coffee, friendly banter, and discussions about the plans for the day, she grabbed her purse, leaving Megan and Garrett on Collin's detail. Collin walked her to the door. His hand caressed her arm. "Sara, call Sanchez and call this off. I can't let you go through with this."

Even though Collin asked her not to go through with it, there wasn't any stopping the plans she had set in motion. The picture would go live in forty-five minutes and, if she wasn't at the mall, then she might miss her opportunity. "Don't you want your life back?"

Collin rubbed the stubble on his chin. "Not at your expense. We can find another way."

She shook her head and placed her palm on his arm. She wanted to give him some peace in his life; she needed to. "There isn't another way. She's after me, so we're going to use it to our advantage on our own terms. Haven't you ever heard that the best defense is a good offense? Well, that's what this is. Marco has another team that will be watching us, and I've got two of the best agents a girl could ask for watching my back. I'll be fine."

Unable to resist, she stretched up on her toes and pressed a quick kiss on his cheek. "Garrett and Megan have the lead while I'm gone. If you need anything, just ask them." She turned to walk out but stopped and spun around. "Try not to give them trouble. They're just doing their job."

She left him standing at the door, and he watched them leave until they reached the security gate. Every fiber in her being told her that he'd be fine without her. It was now Sara that the stalker wanted; she would need to get Sara out of the way for the stalker to truly have Collin. Yes, her plan was for the best, or at least she hoped so.

Lexi glanced up in the rearview mirror. "I have to admit your plan is kind of ballsy."

"Then hand me a bat because I'm going down swinging."

Sara walked into the lingerie store as she simultaneously pulled up Sanchez's website on her phone and verified that the picture had made the home page. Pictures of Collin and her from the fundraiser and the one Sara had planted with herself posing in the lingerie filled the screen. Their scorching kiss from the fundraiser was front and center on the page and made her lips tingle just thinking about it. Heat rose to her cheeks as she felt like a voyeur, even though she was looking at her own pictures. A huge diamond ring had been Photoshopped onto her finger in the picture of them kissing. Sanchez had gone all out on creating just the right atmosphere to piss off the stalker she was trying to taunt. The title on the page made her chuckle. *"This just in....Collin Martin, the World's Most Eligible Bachelor, appears to be off the market. Sara Johnson was seen moments ago at the local mall shopping for lingerie...Could it be for an upcoming honeymoon?"*

Lexi glanced over her shoulder and whistled. "Damn, if I had legs like that, I'd be parading around in skirts all day."

Catherine nudged Lexi's arm. "I bet Trip wouldn't complain."

They both watched as Sara scrolled up and down the screen. "Time to put your game faces on, ladies." They walked farther into the lingerie shop. "It's time to even the score."

Sara tried to pretend to be enjoying herself when, really, her mind was everywhere but on the shopping or enjoying time with her friends. It was just another undercover operation. She was with the best, so why was her gaze darting everywhere. She hadn't heard a thing Catherine or Lexi had said in the last five minutes. No matter which store they entered, her gaze was drawn to the front entrance and everyone around her. Women pushing toddlers in strollers walked nearby. Teenagers and young women laughed and talked in groups as they went about their shopping. No one suspected a criminal probably lurked nearby.

Sara's feet were killing her, her stomach was grumbling, and her mood deteriorated. Maybe this hadn't been such a good plan. Maybe the stalker hadn't even been on the website.

"Well, that was a colossal waste of time," Sara grumbled.

Catherine lifted the bags in her hands. "Shopping is never a waste of time." Her grin grew bigger as she nudged Sara with her arm. "Collin won't be able to keep his hands off you when he gets a peek of the lingerie you bought."

Sara's cheeks reddened as they walked back to the SUV. "You know how this works, Catherine. We aren't sleeping together. He's my assignment." Sara pulled the door open and paused before climbing in. "Oh wait…you two wouldn't understand, would you?"

It wasn't long ago that Lexi married her assignment, or even when Catherine had fallen hard for the client's brother. Shit like that only happened in movies and books or to her extremely lucky best friends, not to someone like Sara.

They all chuckled as they climbed in the vehicle. Only minutes into driving, Lexi announced that they had a tail, and it wasn't one of Marco's team. The tinted windows of the two-door sports car blocked their view of getting an identification on the driver.

"Stalker or senator?" Lexi questioned.

Sara glanced out the back window. "I have no idea."

"What do you want me to do?" Lexi asked as she glanced up in the rearview mirror.

"We need to get her out in the open. Why don't you pull into that park over there?"

Catherine nudged Lexi. "Isn't this the same park where Marco and you cornered Constanza's goons?"

Lexi shrugged. "It's not like it was difficult. They weren't the sharpest crayons in the box."

The park was pretty secluded, but unlike Lexi's encounter, she might not have had Marco hiding in the nearby trees, but she did have her best friends if anything went wrong.

Lexi pulled into the park, and each of them checked their guns before exiting the SUV. The silver sports car drove by once, and just when they thought that maybe Lexi might have been wrong, the car turned back into the lot. To Sara's surprise, Maureen jumped out of the car with a gun in her hand, and it was pointed directly at Sara. "Not so smug now, are you, Sara?"

Maureen's hand trembled as she stepped closer. Her gaze went from Sara's to Lexi's to Catherine's and back again. Maureen waved the gun around. "You two back in the SUV. This is between me and the slut."

Lexi kept her gun trained on Maureen. "Afraid we can't do that. Why don't you drop your weapon, and we can discuss this like adults."

Out of the corner of her eye, Sara spotted the secondary team in the tree line moving into position, and another SUV parking across the road, although no one moved to get out of the car.

This ended here and now. There was no way that Maureen was going to escape. Sara crossed her arms over her chest. "He doesn't love you. Are you that desperate that you have to stalk him?"

Fire flashed in Maureen's eyes as she narrowed them. Her grip on the gun tightened.

Catherine nudged her and spoke under her breath. "Are you sure it's wise to piss off the psycho?"

Sara inched farther away from her friends, trying to keep Maureen's focus solely on her. There was no way she was going to let her friends get hurt. Not today. *Yeah, keep your eyes on me. Just another step...* Maureen glanced over to Lexi, who still had her gun out. Catherine had pulled hers too.

Maureen smirked. "You don't deserve him."

"But I have him," Sara taunted, and Maureen turned her attention back to Sara. "I made him want me all right and, tonight, I'm going to give him what he's been begging me for, and he *has* been begging like a dog wanting a bone."

Sara noticed Maureen's jaw clench before she pulled the trigger. The loud sound of a gunfire shot ricocheted though the air as Sara dodged to the side. The bullet grazed her arm, right where the middle of her chest had been seconds before.

Sara landed with a thud against the asphalt, knocking the breath from her lungs. She'd wanted to talk some sense into the woman without violence. Even though Sara hadn't pulled her gun out, her best friends had her covered. She hadn't expected the woman to fire the gun. Honestly, she didn't think Maureen had the balls to pull the trigger. She'd almost underestimated the woman into an early grave. She whipped her own gun out of the band of her jeans just as another shot rang out in the early evening air.

Lexi was standing over Maureen. She kicked Maureen's gun out of her reach. Sara rolled to her back, trying to catch her breath and whispered her thanks to the main man upstairs or the guardian angel that had watched over them while a member from the other team was on the phone with the police.

Lexi was applying pressure to the wound in Maureen's arm, the same arm she'd been using to hold the gun.

Maureen was wailing like a baby, as if she'd been shot through the chest.

"Oh, shut it, you'll survive." Lexi balked.

Catherine extended her hand and pulled Sara up. Her friend examined Sara's arm even as they heard the sirens in the distance. The second Carrington-Hill team emerged from the cover of the trees.

Police cars screeched to a halt with their sirens blaring. The sheriff stepped out of his cruiser. His gaze traveled over the chaos around him. His deputies had their guns drawn and pointed at the Carrington-Hill team. He held up his arms. "Sara, tell your men to put their weapons away."

Sara nodded and the armed team holstered their weapons. The sheriff stepped over to Sara.

"She tried to kill me, and I want to press charges."

He gestured his men toward Maureen. "Get her some medical attention, and then I want her cuffed and hauled in."

"Why don't you let the paramedics bandage you up? I'll meet you down at the station for your statement while my forensic team processes the site."

Sara glanced up across the road. The other SUV that had been witness to the shootout was no longer in sight. She turned in a circle, looking to see if she could spot the SUV, but it was nowhere to be found.

**\*\*\*\***

Sara walked into the buzzing police station, filled with deputies processing reports and cuffed criminals sitting in chairs on opposite sides of the desk. The sheriff's daughter sat behind the counter with the phone pressed to her ear. She took one look at Sara and raised a brow before dismissing the person on the other end of the phone.

"Oh my god, are you okay?" Katrina asked as her gaze went down the cuts and scrapes on Sara's body.

Sara took a deep breath. The last thing she wanted to do was explain what happened. "I'm here to give my statement. Your dad is expecting me."

The doors to the station burst open, and Collin stomped in with Garrett and Megan right behind him. Collin ran a hand through his already disheveled hair. His gaze scanned the room until it landed on her. He moved through the room and pulled her into his arms. She winced from the pressure on the bandaged cut.

He eased his hold and turned her arm to get a better look. "Are you all right? Do I need to take you to the hospital?"

His genuine concern was endearing and reminded her of what she was missing, not being in a relationship for so long. The smoldering blue of his eyes deepened as he assessed the rest of her body, as if checking to make sure she wasn't hurt any place else.

"The paramedics already checked me out. I'm just here to give my statement and press charges." She placed a reassuring hand on his arm, not sure how he was going to take the news that his publicist would be transferred to the jail after her little stint at the hospital. She dropped her arm. "Wait, how did you know?"

She glanced to Garrett. He gave a slight shake of his head.

"The sheriff called me. What happened?"

"Maureen tried to kill me."

His eyes widened as she recounted what happened at the park. "She's in the hospital with a gunshot wound to the arm. I suspect that, after they treat her, she'll be going to jail."

Katrina mumbled something under her breath, Sara turned. "Excuse me."

Katrina shrugged. "Nothing, I'm just glad you're okay."

The sheriff headed toward them, like a man on a mission. He extended a hand. "We really need to quit meeting like this."

"Sheriff," Collin said in way of greeting.

"This shouldn't take too long, Sara. I just need to get your official statement."

Sara glanced over at Garrett, who was unusually silent. "Garrett, please take Collin home, and I'll be there when I can."

Garrett nodded before the sheriff escorted Sara down the long hall and into a sterile interrogation room. The bare room had nothing more than a long desk and a couple of chairs. The sheriff pulled out a seat across from her, and Sara proceeded over the next hour to give him her accounting of what had transpired. Maureen most likely will be doing jail time for attempted murder.

"Do you think Maureen was Collin's stalker?"

Sara shrugged at his question. "Everything points to Maureen. To be honest, she was really sloppy. I don't think she has the street smarts to pull any of this off. I still think we're dealing with someone else."

The sheriff leaned back in his chair and crossed his arms over his chest as they debated the subject. "It's possible she just snapped. You did say that Collin fired her, and you and her tussled in that hotel room. Maybe it was enough to send her over the edge, and she wasn't thinking clearly."

Sara let his words mull around in her mind. It did make sense, but still she had a gut feeling that Collin's woes weren't over with yet. "I'd need to see proof to buy into the idea that Maureen is the stalker. It's still too soon to let our guard down."

The sheriff stood. "We'll get a search warrant for her place and let you know if we turn up anything that points to her as being Collin's stalker."

Sara nodded and held out her hand. "I also have some questions for her, if you can arrange for me to see her."

He nodded. "I'll see what I can do."

"Thank you for your help."

# 13 CHAPTER

Exhausted from a day of shopping and an hour of interrogation, Sara arrived back at Collin's at nine o'clock that night with one thing on her mind—a nice soak in a tub to ease the soreness in her arm and to rinse away the dirt from her body. She eased down the long driveway in the SUV that Lexi had left for her at the sheriff's office. Cars littered the front of the mansion. Worse yet, they were cars she recognized. Not only was Marco's shiny BMW parked out front, but her father's SUV was there as well. It wasn't bad enough that she had to deal with Maureen, but her boss and her father too? All in the same twenty-four-hour period?

She parked next to the SUV and killed the ignition. She gripped the steering wheel tight one last time before she blew out an annoyed breath, exited the SUV, and headed right into the line of fire for the second time that day.

Garrett walked out of the house and down the stairs. As he approached, he had a look of pity on his face. "I wouldn't go in there if I were you. It's getting pretty heated."

She didn't have time to ask for details before the door flung open again. Her father stood in the doorway. The hard lines on his face told her exactly what she was walking into. She walked up the steps holding her chin up. "Hi, Dad."

His gaze landed on the bright white bandage secured around her arm, and his scowl deepened. "You've got some explaining to do, little miss."

She lifted a brow. Maybe had she worn the damn coat, she could have hidden the wound but she'd never hidden from anything before and she'd be damned if she was going to start now.

"Maybe you'd like to explain about being forced off the road, or how about the fact that your tires were slashed?" He crossed his arms over his chest, "Or maybe you want to start by explaining what you have on the senator."

Sara couldn't help but roll her eyes. The old man meant well, even though she didn't want to recount what had happened for what seemed like the hundredth time. She walked up to him, placed a kiss on his cheek, and patted his arm as she side-stepped him into the house. "It's all part of the job, Dad. I'm fine. Why don't you go home?"

The door shut behind her, and she didn't have to glance over her shoulder to know that the stubborn man hadn't left like she suggested. Seemed her bath was going to have to wait a little longer.

Loud voices came from the direction of the kitchen, and she let out a long sigh. It appeared that her only quick escape route to the pool house was cut off. There was no way the men in that room would let her leave until she settled whatever the argument was about.

All talking ceased as she walked into the room. Collin's face was red with anger. Drew had his arms crossed over his chest, and Marco had his arms placed on the table with his head lowered as if exhausted.

"Care to fill me in so I can take sides?"

"Always with a smart remark. You haven't changed one bit. I would have thought that being shot at would bring you to your senses," her father said as he strolled by her and over to the coffee pot.

"What can I say? I learned from the best."

Sara patted Marco on the back as she followed her father to the coffee pot. To her disbelief, he held out a mug for her. She smiled, knowing that no matter how mad her father was, he always took care of her. "Thanks, Dad."

He nodded.

She turned back to the rest of the room full of silent men. "What did I miss?"

Marco stood and crossed his arms over his chest. "Just a disagreement. Seems our client here wants to take you out of the line of fire, and I'm trying to persuade him that it's a bad idea."

Sara swallowed the scalding coffee along with the flash of hurt from the statement. After everything that had happened, did Collin not see that she was damn capable of doing her job? Her hurt quickly turned into anger. She turned to her father. "Whose side are you on?"

Her dad raised his brow. "Do you even have to ask?"

She gave a slight nod. She already knew there was no way in hell that daddy dearest would want his little girl in danger. "Two votes for Collin." She looked at Drew. "And you?"

Drew gave her his dazzling smile. "I don't think Collin is thinking straight. I'm on your side."

"You don't know what the hell you're talking about Drew. If you were truly on her side, you wouldn't want to see her get hurt and you'd want her off the case too." Collin argued.

Drew shrugged. "She knows what she's doing; I'm still on her side."

She gave another nod of acknowledgement before she turned to Marco, who's vote, along with her own, was really the only one in the room that mattered. "What about you? Are you worried for my safety and do you think Collin's threat has truly been eliminated?"

He shook his head. "I'm always worried about your safety but, no, I don't believe the threat is gone. Once we have the proof from the search warrant on Maureen's place, then I might change my mind but, right now, it doesn't add up. All we have right now is a jilted lover, with bad aim, that seems to be trigger happy. If ballistics can match the bullets found from the murder scenes with Maureen's gun, then I'll pull you from the investigation, but not until then."

Finally, a rational comment that she agreed with, one that wasn't pitted against whether she was capable of doing her job or worry for her safety. She turned to Collin and tried to keep a straight face as she spoke. "Seems you've been outvoted, big guy, three to two. It looks like I'm staying on assignment for a little while longer. Not that the votes would have deterred me from staying."

Collin threw his arms up. "I'm the paying customer here. My vote should have more weight."

Sara shrugged. Even though Collin's statement was true, she knew that Marco would do the right thing. It was encoded in his DNA, just like it was in hers. "Money or no money, I'm not comfortable dropping my detail until the job is done, and I have a gut feeling that this isn't over."

Drew placed a palm on Collin's shoulder. "What's the harm in waiting for the evidence?"

Collin shrugged off his brother's palm and pointed at Sara. "She took a bullet and could have been killed. I won't let her do that again…to protect me." He shook his head and stomped from the room as he called over his shoulder. "You're fired, Sara."

As if his words were going to make her leave. She glanced at Marco, who shook his head. Drew threw his arm around her shoulder and gave a gentle squeeze. "He'll come around to his senses by morning. He was just worried about you."

Sara balled her fists at her sides. The stubborn man was going to drive her to drink and, if he thought he could get rid of her that easily, the man had a thing or two to learn. She placed a smile on her face and headed toward the same door that

Collin had disappeared through. She turned under the threshold. "I'm sure you can all see yourselves out."

Marco grinned, her father frowned, and Drew chuckled. Her father placed his mug in the sink and stormed past her. "Your mother is expecting you for dinner next Saturday night. I expect you to be in attendance, with or without a date."

The front door slammed as she spun on her heel and took the stairs two at a time up the banister toward Collin's room. Their conversation was anything but over. She didn't have butterflies in her stomach. No, she had demons to exorcize, starting with telling Collin what a jackass he was being.

Under normal circumstances, she would have knocked on his door, but these weren't normal circumstances. She had something to say, damn it, and he was going to hear it whether he wanted to or not. She shoved his bedroom door open and stalked into the huge room. Collin stood at the window with his back toward the rest of the room. She didn't waste time appreciating the expanse of his personal space.

"You hired me to pretend to be your girlfriend so we could catch a killer. I'm a trained professional, not some bimbo that can't take care of herself." Her cheeks felt like they were on fire, not from embarrassment but from anger, anger that he was foolish enough to think she'd go along with whatever he wanted. "I knew what I was getting into the moment I agreed to your assignment, and I thought you were smart enough to realize it too... I guess I was wrong."

He spun around and advanced on her, grabbing her arms. He lifted the bandaged one. "This…." He wiggled her arm. "This was too close. She could have killed you." He released her and stepped back. "I won't let there be a next time, Sara. I'm sorry you don't understand; I just can't."

Her gaze held his. The intensity in his words, coupled with the tension in the air, sizzled around her. Never in her entire life had she felt this much heat from an argument nor seen such sincerity in someone's eyes. Her shoulders relaxed, and the heat in her chest evaporated. The man cared and, not only that, all of his passion was aimed at her. She covered the distance he was trying to put between them, no longer interested in keeping Collin at arm's length. No, she wanted this man, now more than ever. His gaze searched her face before landing on her lips. She licked her lips, wishing it was his tongue instead of her own. She reached for him and crushed her lips to his. It wasn't nice; it wasn't sweet. It was demanding and rough. It was everything she felt for Collin. She didn't hold back. She pressed her body against his as she ran her fingers through his hair. He only hesitated for a mere second before joining in with the same ferocity.

Buttons started popping, and clothes were discarded at a pace neither one of them was willing to change until they were both completely naked.

"Commando…I would have pegged you as a boxer guy." Sara giggled.

She wanted him and by the looks of his jutting erection, he wanted her just as much, and she wouldn't deny either of them another second. This wasn't a slow coupling between two people. This was raw and dirty, and it turned her on in every way. His hands explored down the length of her spine as his hardened erection pressed against her belly. He cupped her butt and lifted her in the air as he moved to press her back against the wall. His cock was pressed at the juncture of her thighs, but he'd yet to break the barrier. She was wet and wild for him. She wanted him to fill her. No, she needed him to fill her. She locked her legs around his waist.

He pulled his lips from hers. His breathing came out in quick pants that matched her own. "Are you sure?"

No words came to her lips. All she could do was nod.

He leaned his forehead against hers and tried to slow down. "We should stop and use protection. I'm clean, but I don't want to get you pregnant."

She shook her head and squirmed in his hold, trying to align their bodies. "I'm clean too and on the pill."

His gaze searched her face. No longer willing to wait, she latched on to his lips and kissed him with the same wild frenzy she felt down in her core.

He pressed her shoulders into the wall and aligned their bodies before surging upward and into her, eliciting a gasp from her. He stood still and buried his head in the crook of her neck and let out a guttural moan. "Oh God, you feel good. Just like I knew you would."

Unable to wait longer, she nudged him with her heels. "Collin, please. I need more."

Collin slowly slid out from her and rammed home again. His pace quickened with each thrust. Every nerve ending in her body was strung tight and tightened further as he plunged his cock in and out of her, grazing her clit as he moved. She felt the stirring of her orgasm and knew she wouldn't be able to last. Her tongue dueled with the same urgency, matching their movements. Her orgasm hit her hard and fast. She came, screaming his name, not caring if anyone left in the house heard her cries.

He kissed her neck and thrust two more times before letting out a deep groan in the crook of her neck. Their sweat-soaked bodies glistened as if they'd just run a marathon. She enjoyed this type of workout a whole hell of a lot better than doing laps in the pool.

He kept her pinned against the wall. Only when his breathing slowed did he finally raise his head. His blue eyes were clouded, but he'd yet to pull out or release her. "Next time I take you, it will be slow and on the bed."

He pulled out of her and let her slowly slide down his body, keeping his arms around her until her legs became more stable. "Next time I let you take me, I'll be wet and in the shower. Speaking of which…" She walked toward the bathroom. "Care to wash my hard-to-reach spots?"

He appeared behind her as she turned on the water. He turned her in his arms and placed a gentle kiss on her lips. "This doesn't change the fact that I still want you off my case."

Sara rested her palms against the hard planes of his chest. "And this doesn't change the fact that I don't care."

He smacked her butt with his hand. "Are you always this difficult?"

She shrugged and stepped into the tub. "No….normally worse." She grinned. "Care to come in and find out?"

# 14 CHAPTER

A noise in the dark, unfamiliar room woke Sara from a sound sleep. Collin's arm, pressed against her stomach, pulled her closer. She heard the sound again and, now awake, recognized the noise immediately. Her phone, that had been in the back pocket of her jeans, was vibrating. She slid out from beneath Collin's arm and searched through the darkened room until she found her jeans and pulled the phone from the pocket. She flicked the phone open. The bright light of the screen made her squint as she glanced back at the bed to make sure the light hadn't woken Collin up.

Satisfied she hadn't woken him, she glanced at the missed call and the accompanying text from

Marco. "Call back ASAP. If I don't hear from you in the next ten minutes, I'm sending the security detail to wake you."

Sara threw on Collin's discarded shirt and moved to the privacy of the bathroom. She redialed Marco's number. He picked up on the first ring. "This better be important. It's only four a.m."

"Sara, Maureen has escaped from the hospital."

Sara let out a string of curse words. "How? I thought she was in police custody. Didn't they have her guarded?"

"I don't have all of the details yet, but it looks like she had help. The handcuffs were hanging from the rails of the bed. Someone must have slipped her the key or helped her escape. I have agents on the scene along with the sheriff."

Sara rubbed her eyes as she tried to make sense of the mess. "Any news from ballistics or from the search? Did they find anything in her apartment?"

"No word back from ballistics, but they did find another gun, some scissors, and a newspaper that was cut up sitting out on her dining room table."

Sara sat down on the closed commode. Even half asleep, she still didn't feel Maureen was the stalker. Even though she couldn't pinpoint the problem, something didn't add up. Maybe it was because Maureen had help in escaping, and stalkers generally liked to work alone. "I get the feeling it's a setup. Why did she have two guns?"

"Me too. It's all too neat and tidy, like it was staged. I want you to make sure the guys are on high alert until she's recaptured."

She nodded as though Marco could see her. There was a rap on the door. "Are you okay? Who are you talking to?"

She pulled the bathroom door open and Collin stood under the archway, wiping the sleep from his eyes. "Everything okay, baby?"

Was she? Hell no, she wasn't okay. The stalker was still on the loose and now had an accomplice. Not only one person was out to kill her but two. "Marco, I'll call you back."

She didn't wait for Marco to reply before she flipped her phone closed and stood. "We have a problem."

She walked out of the bathroom and switched on the bedside lamp before she started to rummage through the pile of clothing on the floor in search of her clothes, socks, and shoes.

"Isn't it one that can wait until morning?" He pulled her into his arms and kissed her. "If the house isn't burning down, you can wait. Why don't you come back to bed so we can talk about it and pick up where we left off?"

The man was insatiable, not that she could get enough of him either. But now wasn't the time to forget where she was or her job. No, now was the time for action, for making plans and keeping Collin safe. She pressed a kiss to his lips and stepped around him, sitting on the bed to pull on her socks and shoes.

"As much as I would love too, I can't. Maureen's escaped from the hospital, and it appears as though she had help."

Collin moved to the closet and slid into a pair of jeans. "What the hell do you mean she's escaped? And who the hell would have helped her?"

"Someone uncuffed her. Marco has a team on-site, but I need to do a perimeter check and meet with my team." She tried for her best I'm-not-worried-and-neither-should-you-be voice and failed miserably.

He lowered to his knees between her legs. "Sara, please don't go."

She cupped his cheek. "I'll be fine. I promise." She leaned over, opened the bedside drawer and grabbed her gun which she'd stuffed away last night, right next to his. She shoved the revolver into the waistband in the back of her jeans. She pulled his gun out and handed it to him. "Just in case, remember?"

He placed the gun on the bed and kissed her with the same searing heat she remembered from hours ago. "Is there any way I can talk you into staying with me? What if we go away together, somewhere tropical, just the two of us? While the others figure this out."

She leaned her forehead against his. "As great as that sounds. I want to give you your life back." She stood and walked to the door before turning around one more time to look at him. "And that's damn sure what I'm going to do."

Sara made quick work of returning to the pool house, grabbing her comm, and donning her shoulder holster with guns locked and loaded. She could only hope that Maureen, and whoever had helped her escape, showed up. Every sound had her nerves strung tight. The team and she checked the perimeter, and she briefed them on the latest development, along with passing out Maureen's photo.

The only threat without a face was the stalker. She found Collin in the kitchen cooking when she returned. He took one look at her face, poured her a mug of coffee, and handed it to her. He was barefoot and hadn't even brushed his hair. It was a sight that she wouldn't mind waking up to every morning. "What are you doing?"

He grinned and slid the eggs onto a platter next to the already heaping mounds of bacon. "Cooking…I had to do something. The waiting is driving me crazy."

Sara plucked a piece of bacon from the pile as she radioed the teams that Collin had cooked, demanding that one crew would be taking their food back out to their station while the rest ate inside. "You know…you're safe here. They'd be stupid to make a move with so many guards on the premises." Sara hopped up onto the counter, her legs dangling over the side. "I've been thinking."

He turned off the stove and moved between her legs. "That's dangerous. I'm not going to like this, am I?"

She worried her bottom lip. "Probably not."

\*\*\*\*

Any appetite Collin had worked up, vanished when Sara said she'd been thinking. From the looks of it, her thoughts weren't the typical morning-after thoughts he'd expect her to have. He had to restrain himself from plucking her off the counter and turning all cave man on her by hauling her back upstairs where he could keep her safe and out of harm's way.

He watched as she chewed on the pink flesh of her bottom lip, the little telltale sign that she was working something out in her mind. Collin brushed the pad of his thumb over her swollen lip before replacing it with his lips. He wanted to savor the few stolen moments between them, unsure if they would even have more when this was all over. Words were left unspoken, thanks to the call she'd had this morning.

She broke the kiss and hopped off the counter. "We can't do this here. The team will be here any second."

As if on cue, they started piling into the kitchen, grabbing plates and loading them with pancakes, eggs, sausage, and bacon.

Collin stepped out of the way of the hungry men and moved to Sara's side. "What were you thinking?"

She shook her head. "It's not important." She shrugged. "Besides, I still need to run it by Marco."

He leaned in close to her ear. The smell of her jasmine shampoo tickled his nose. Such a delicate flower, so unlike the strong woman wearing it. The same stubborn woman he found himself drawn to. "Don't make any brash decisions."

She glanced up at him and rolled her eyes. "I wouldn't dream of it."

Yeah, sure she wouldn't. Just like he wouldn't worry about her when she went off half-cocked on whatever great idea she thought she had. No, not his Sara. *His? Where the hell did that come from?* The more time he spent with her, the more he was finding out that she was irresistible, not to mention sex personified. Yeah, he could get used to having her around if he could keep her alive long enough to ease her into the idea of having a relationship with him. He'd have his hands full trying to talk the stubborn woman out of doing anything crazy...as if that was even possible.

Twenty minutes went by before Marco let himself into Collin's house. He snapped at the men sitting around the table, not liking the skeleton crew stationed around the property. They all scurried and, after dumping their dishes in the sink, reported back to their posts.

"What did you expect Marco, they needed food?"

He harrumphed as Collin offered Marco a mug of coffee and joined him and Sara at the table. There was no way he was being left out of this conversation. Collin laid his arm across the back of Sara's chair. Marco's gaze watched the entire rookie move as though it was a first date and he was in a movie theater and pretended to yawn. His actions didn't go unnoticed by Marco or Sara, but neither one of them mentioned it. Marco's brow hitched as he glanced back and forth between Collin and Sara. It was time everyone knew what he'd just figured out himself.

"Tell me you found something on the surveillance video from the hospital."

Marco tossed a file on the table. Sara opened it, and Collin looked over her shoulder. A figure could be seen pulling back the partition curtain to the adjoining makeshift room in the bay of the ER. The deputies on duty were chatting it up with a brunette nurse, not even paying attention to what was going on.

"It's the same person from the hotel." She glanced up. "Why is Collin's stalker helping Maureen?"

Collin had a feeling that he knew the answer to that question, even if Sara hadn't figured it out yet in her head. They both had a few things in common. They both wanted to kill Sara as was evident by the new bandage she had wrapped around her arm.

"Oh I don't know… maybe because they both want to see you dead." Collin sarcastically answered her question.

"Sara love," Marco said, "the question you should be asking isn't why, but how."

*Sara love.* Collin didn't like the sound of endearment coming from her boss, but now wasn't the time to discuss it. He pushed it to the back of his mind. "How did the stalker know about Maureen's arrest? I looked in this morning's paper. It wasn't even listed yet, and it hasn't been mentioned on the morning news. How is it even possible?"

"I bet I know." Sara pulled her phone out of her pocket and pulled up Sanchez's blog. "Well, that didn't take long."

She handed the phone to Marco before he passed it to Collin. Sitting on the home page of his blog was a grainy picture that was taken in the park where the shooting had taken place. It was a picture of Maureen being handcuffed and stuffed into an ambulance. The caption read; *If you can't beat them...just shoot them?*

Collin rubbed his hand through his hair as he handed the phone back to Sara. He wished he'd never even pulled her into his mess. His gut clenched as a feeling of dread settled over him. Maybe he should have tried to deal with his stalker himself. Marco rose from the table. "I think it's time to pay the blogger a visit. Maybe he can shed some light on who he thinks the stalker might be."

He turned to leave but stopped and glanced over his shoulder. "Oh, I forgot to tell you. The FBI is looking for the senator to question him about Natasha's murder, and he's vanished."

Sara bit her bottom lip. Collin didn't care how the FBI figured it out. He was just glad that the senator was being dealt with.

"How did they even know to link Natasha and the Senator together?"

Marco grinned. "A picture is worth a thousand words, luv." Marco shrugged. "The Senator is on the run and probably far too busy trying to stay one step ahead of the FBI to even worry about you. You've got enough on your plate."

Sara rose out of her seat. "Marco..."

He held up a hand, effectively stopping what she was about to say. The set of his jaw tightened. "It's time to resort to Plan B."

Collin glanced between the both of them. "What's Plan B?"

Sara wouldn't even look at him. She lowered her head. "I agree, I was thinking the same thing."

She left Marco and Collin standing at the table in the kitchen. He didn't like the sound of Plan B. Hell, she needed the guards just as much as he did, if not worse. The stalker and Maureen weren't trying to kill him like they were Sara.

Marco excused himself. No one gave Collin an official answer on what Plan B might be, but he'd figured it out. Oh, this wasn't going to work. She didn't want to be removed from the case and now she was just up and leaving him, just as things were getting heated between them. He rubbed his aching chest and swallowed around the lump in his throat. He wouldn't let her; he'd talk her out of it. He had to. He wasn't going to let her walk into more danger, danger that was his fault. No, not her too.

He leaned against the open door of the pool house and watched as she repacked her suitcase. He moved to the bed and plopped down. "Sara, what is Plan B?"

"Plan B is taking me off your immediate detail. They've bought the bait and now I'm more of a liability than anything else. We both knew that the threat might turn in my direction, and you're in more danger if I stay. They'll still come after me because I'll make sure that it's evident we're still a couple; I'm not backing down. I'm going to call them out, but I can't be distracted for even a second and let's face it Collin... you're a distraction. The only other option is to put you in a safe house and

I'll stay here and deal with the threat. Either way, I need you out of the picture."

"How long are we talking?"

Sara shrugged. "I don't know. I guess until we find Maureen and catch your stalker. They'll both try to take me out of the equation before coming back for you."

Collin propped himself up with his elbow as he lay back on the bed and mulled over how he might talk her into staying. "How are we going to play this? You're my girlfriend, pretend or not, and the reporters are going to want answers for your absence. It's not like I can show up at the charity functions without you. Let me rephrase that… I won't show up at the charity functions without you."

Sara zipped up her suitcase and did one more walk-through of the room and adjoining bathroom before she returned and sat next to him. "Yes, you will."

Collin sat up, took her hand and kissed her palm. "Don't go."

Sara slid her fingers from his and stood. She clicked the comm in her ear. "10-4."

"Garrett just arrived to replace me. Collin, you won't be helping anyone if you're dead. Maureen might not kill you, but one wrong word to your stalker, and she could turn on you. You need to be smart about this." She cupped his cheek. "Please stay safe."

He stood and was about to rebuff her remark before she leaned up on her toes and kissed him. She kissed him like she'd never see him again, a final good-bye kiss, sweet and tender, yet heated and sincere all at the same time. A tear trickled down her cheek as she picked up her bag and, without another word, left him standing in the pool house.

Oh no, this wouldn't work at all. By the time he realized what she'd just done and he'd run up to the main house, she was gone.

# 15 CHAPTER

Sara arrived back at her house to find Lexi and Catherine waiting on her porch. Three peas in a pod if you didn't count for the differences in their love lives. She should have known that they'd show up with a gallon of her favorite ice cream and margarita mix. Their tradition of comforting each other wasn't lost on her, and she did need comforting. She wasn't as worried about the threats to her life as she was the man she'd left behind. The man that was better off without her. So many unsaid conversations they needed to have. She reminded herself it was for the best. Being away from him might help to keep him safe, no matter how much she hated just picking up and leaving when things between them weren't settled.

"Looks like you're stuck with us until this is all over."

Catherine grabbed the bag out of Sara's trunk as Lexi threw her arm around Sara's shoulder and steered her up the steps to her empty, lonely house. "You know this isn't necessary."

Catherine patted her on the back. "Sure it is. We're not going to let any deranged women take a potshot at you. We'll always have your back, just like you would for us."

Lexi followed into the house behind Sara. "Besides, it's our duty as your best friends..." She glanced over her shoulder at Catherine. "Speaking of which...I think it's time for a visit to the beach house. Nothing will give you a better prospective like the salt water, sand, and sun."

Sara smiled and knew it didn't reach her eyes. It felt like there was a big gaping hole in her chest where her heart normally sat. The uncertainty of the outcome weighed heavy on her shoulders. Her mind was scattered, but she was determined. Her friends were trying to take her out of the danger just like she'd done with Collin and she appreciated that... but it wasn't going to change a thing.

"I'm sure you can last a week without Mr. God's-gift-to-women, right?" Catherine asked as she set the bag down.

Sara felt the heat travel up to her cheeks just thinking about Collin and their last night together. They'd had sex more than any one couple should be allowed.

Lexi gasped and covered her mouth. "Oh no, you didn't." She turned to Catherine. "She's been holding out on us." Lexi pointed to Sara. "She slept with the client."

Catherine winked. "Was he good?"

Sara waved her hand as she walked to the fridge and pulled out a soda. "Oh, give me a break, will ya? At least I didn't marry him. Even if you did have a great reason, I'm still not sure I could have done that."

Catherine threw her head back and laughed. It wasn't too long ago that Lexi had staged a real marriage to Trip to figure out who was behind his corporate embezzlement and who the culprit was who had attempted to murder Catherine when she was working undercover. During the marriage, no matter how much of a sham it was originally, feelings developed, love bloomed and the upcoming wedding was going to be real in less than a month.

"Sure you would have. Lexi just beat you to the punch, and who can blame her? Have you seen how hot her billionaire husband is? He's one hunk of a fine specimen."

Lexi had the grace to blush, even as they all plopped down on the couches in Sara's living room. "I appreciate it, guys, but this isn't necessary. I'm sure that Marco has a team watching me, and you two have lives to get back to."

After arguing for two hours, Sara walked them both to the door and waved as they pulled away. Her gaze went to the SUV parked across the street. One of Marco's teams, she was sure.

Sara checked all of her windows, locked the door, set the alarm, and knowing the team was inconspicuously stationed around the perimeter of her house, she curled up on the sofa with a gun under the cushion and a book she'd been dying to read. She normally longed for the quietness of her house, but not tonight. Her thoughts were on Collin.

Her cell phone rang, and she was glad for the reprieve from the silence. She went to her dining room table and flipped it open. "Johnson."

"He's been shot," Marco said matter-of-factly.

"Excuse me?" Her heart stuttered, her legs turned to jelly, and she sagged against her dining room table. No, no, no, she'd left Collin to keep him safe. This wasn't happening; this wasn't how it was all supposed to go down. She was grabbing her keys from her purse and had almost made it to the door before Marco elaborated.

"Sanchez, the blogger, has been shot but, since it wasn't through the heart like the stalker's other victims, I'm thinking it was Maureen that came for him."

Her heartbeat started to return to normal. Just the mere thought of something happening to Collin had her head spinning. Maybe leaving him hadn't been such a good idea after all. At least she would have been extra eyes to keep him safe. "Is he dead?"

"No, but he is unconscious, and based on the untouched breakfast he left on the stove, I'm betting he was shot early this morning. We're lucky he didn't bleed out. Sara…" The tone of Marco's voice when said her first name told her she wasn't going to like what was coming next.

So she cut him off. "No, I'm not running; I'm not hiding, and I'm damn sure not going on vacation *or* staying with you. What else do you have?"

"How do you want to play this?"

"Let's narrow the stalker down. What time did Sanchez upload the picture of Maureen being arrested onto the computer?"

"Hang on a second." Sara heard the clicking of the keyboard. "It looks like he downloaded the picture at seven a.m., but he uploaded the post at nine a.m."

Sara plopped down in her recliner. "Why did he wait so long to post it?" Her mind raced with possible scenarios. She rushed to the table and flipped open the file with the pictures that Marco had given her earlier at Collin's house. The time stamp on the back read seven-thirty."

Sara bit her lip. "Okay, so we can narrow down who knew about the arrest. The picture wasn't posted until after Sanchez was shot, so his stalker had to have been someone who knew what was going on even before the picture went live. If I had to guess, the stalker came back and shot Sanchez, trying to pin it on Maureen, although I'm not sure why since the stalker was the one who freed her."

The line went silent. "You think it was an inside job?"

"I think it was either someone he knew or someone who knew what was going on. That narrows it down to Collin, everyone at his house, our team, and anyone I would have seen at the police department. We're going to need background checks on everyone, including the criminals at the station that day. Also cross-reference those names with the roster from the cancer benefit. That should really narrow down our list and give us a good start on suspects."

"It's going to take a while to tap into their database and run the checks. How do you want to play this in the mean time?"

"The bitches want me, so let's send them both a message."

Marco chuckled. "What do you have in mind, luv?"

A knock sounded on her door. A knock she hadn't been expected. "Someone's at the door. Let me call you back."

"Sara... be careful."

She flipped her phone closed, moved to the foyer on silent feet, pulled the drawer open, and grabbed the Berretta that she had stashed on the underside of the drawer. She stood on her tiptoes and glanced through the peephole.

"You've got to be kidding me." She hit the buttons on the security code, flipped the lock, and pulled the door open with a jerk. "What the hell are you doing here? Do you have a death wish?"

"He doesn't deserve this, and neither do you. Tell me what I can do to help." Collin's assistant, Regina, barged in with a black backpack thrown over her shoulder. "The reason Collin hired me is because of my expertise at keeping track of not only his schedule but the small details. I think I might have something to help you track down where Maureen might be holed up."

That gut feeling of fight or flight never registered with Sara. She didn't view Regina as a threat, although with a bag that hadn't been checked, she probably should have. "What's in the bag?"

Regina unzipped it and pulled out a one-inch binder and handed it to Sara. "A copy of every deal that Maureen has made that included Collin, along with a list of all of her properties and known acquaintances." Regina dropped the bag by the table and walked into the kitchen, only returning a few minutes later with two coffee mugs in her hand. "Ms. Johnson, I see a lot, I know a lot, and I can help you. Maureen has her own personal assistant, and we're friends. If I was a betting woman, I would bet money that she doesn't return to any of her properties, but she'll use what she knows. And that would point to Collin's rarely used, untouched residential properties. The police wouldn't be smart enough to look at those places."

Sara took the mug that Regina handed her and moved to the dining room table where she could spread out the file. Regina grabbed her laptop from the bag and booted it. Her fingers flew across the keyboard as she bit her lip with a determination Sara had only ever seen in herself and her friends. This woman meant business, and she might be the best person to help Carrington-Hill track down Maureen.

A few hours went by and two pots of coffee vanished. Sara was no closer to figuring out where

Maureen might be hiding than before Regina showed up. Regina was seated at the end of the table, clicking away on the keyboard, trying to figure out where Maureen might be holed up. She stopped suddenly and gasped. "The server just went down." She started clicking furiously on the keyboard before she leaned back in her chair and looked up at Sara. "I don't understand."

Sara stood and grabbed her keys while hunched over the table. She ran her fingertip down the list of properties associated with Collin but couldn't find what she was looking for. "What would you do to hurt the man who turned on you?"

Regina shrugged. "Hurt him where it counts, I guess."

Sara grinned like a child that had found her favorite doll. "Exactly. I assume he doesn't keep his server on his property."

Regina rounded the table and pointed to an address in the business district about ten minutes away. "He, along with several other techies, keeps them secure at Global Tech, but there is no way she could have gotten past the security they keep onsite. They wouldn't have even let her in without a clearance badge. And they only give those to the people that store onsite."

Sara tore the address from the binder. "Do you have a badge?"

"Well, yes. Mr. Martin gave me a badge in the event I ever needed to go there on his behalf. You know in case something happened when he was out of town and the situation couldn't wait for him to get back."

"I'll bet he gave Maureen one too. I need your badge."

Regina reached into her purse, opened her wallet, and pulled out the badge, handing it to Sara. For the first time since returning home, Sara held a sliver of hope that she could take at least one of the psychos out of the equation. Sara grabbed her keys, her Beretta, and then Regina's arm, and escorted her to the door and one of the security details SUV across the street. She pulled open the back passenger door and helped Regina inside. Megan and Dixon, another Carrington-Hill investigator, were in the front seats. "Make sure she gets back to Mr. Martin's residence in one piece. I've got a lead on Maureen."

Sara jogged over to her SUV and hopped inside. The butterflies in her stomach summersaulted the closer she drove toward Global Tech. This was the break she needed. Now if only she could catch Maureen on the property, then it would really be time to celebrate. Sara was stopped at a red light when she spotted Maureen in a red four-door sedan taking a right onto the street in front of Sara. *Finally, the stars have aligned, and it's my lucky day.* When the light changed, Sara gunned it, but kept enough distance not to let on that Maureen had a tail. She hit the Bluetooth in her car and waited for Marco to pick up.

"You better have a good reason for sending your detail back to Collin's house. Where the hell are you, Sara?"

"I'm on her six."

"Who's the target, and where are you?"

"I don't have time to explain. Pull up the GPS on my vehicle and send a team to tail me. Maureen is in a red four-door sedan in front of me; I'm tailing her, hoping that she'll lead me right back to the stalker."

"How the hell did you find her?"

Sara shrugged but kept her gaze on the red car, two cars ahead of her. "I had help, and if I'd waited one more second to check it out, I would have missed her turning out of the entrance of Global Tech."

"I'll call the sheriff and have him and his deputies meet us there."

"No!" Sara screamed into the speaker. "I want her handed over to the FBI for holding until we at least clear the staff at the sheriff's department. I don't want her to miraculously escape again."

"Sara, she's dangerous. Don't move in until I get there."

Sara rolled her eyes. "Well then, you better hurry."

Sara heard the rev of the Marco's engine. "I'm on my way."

He disconnected the call. Sara continued to follow Maureen to an address on the outskirts of town, a little house down a dirt road surrounded by trees. Sara recognized the address as one of Collin's properties. Sara bypassed the dirt road and continued farther up the street until she found a decent place off the road to stash her vehicle.

Marco's words replayed in her mind. *Don't move in.* She debated for a half a second and stepped out of the vehicle. She wouldn't go in, but that didn't

mean she couldn't take a look around. Yeah,
scouting the area didn't technically fall under the
category of "moving in on the residence".

KATE ALLENTON

# 16 CHAPTER

Sara tried her best to move on silent feet through the forest that separated her from the house where Maureen was hiding out. Every crack of dead leaves beneath her feet sounded a million times louder in her mind than what it probably was to the untrained ear. Her heart raced in anticipation the closer she maneuvered through the property. For once, Sara felt a glimmer of hope that maybe this would soon be over.

She crouched down behind a large tree trunk and peeked out into the clearing, her gun held steady in her hand. There was no way Maureen was getting out of this, no way Sara would let the bitch do any more harm to Collin than what she'd already done.

A cool breeze nipped the air, eliciting a shiver down her spine. The sun was just starting to set in the evening sky as she observed Maureen moving through the house, passing by several windows. *Only Maureen.* And, just like that, a little bit of her hope subsided, guessing the stalker wouldn't be joining in on the party. Under the cover of night, Marco, she and their team of specialized agents would administer the takedown.

A plan was already forming in her mind when she heard the unmistakable crunch of leaves behind her and Marco appeared by her side and whispered, "I thought I told you to stay in the car."

Sara shook her head. "Nope, you said don't move in on her." She turned and grinned at him. "And I didn't."

Marco rolled his eyes, a move she'd seldom seen him make. She smiled, knowing that the situation was anything but funny. "Where is the rest of the team?"

"Taking up positions surrounding the house. We've got snipers on the front door and a blackout team ready when I give the signal. I don't want you to move from this spot."

Yeah right, as if that is going to happen. She had a different idea of how she wanted this to play out. She wanted to be front and center for the capture. She wanted….no, needed, to let Maureen know that Sara was responsible for her demise. "How about I play bait?"

"How about not."

Sara stuck out her bottom lip. "You're no fun."

Marco shrugged off his bulletproof vest and placed it around Sara before he lifted the binoculars to his eyes. "Shit, she's about to leave."

Unable to remain rooted in the safety of the trees, Sara sprinted out into the open. A disheveled Maureen, wearing jeans and a wrinkled shirt, emerged from the house with the strap of a black bag hefted on her shoulder. They were the same clothes from the attempted murder on Sara's life. The only thing different this time around was that Maureen wasn't hidden behind the steel of a gun. No, this time, Sara had the firepower to her advantage. *Not so lucky this time, are you, Maureen?*

Sara pointed the gun at Maureen and cautiously stepped closer, closing the distance between them. "Drop the bag, Maureen, and put your hands on top of your head. You're surrounded, and the snipers have you in their sights. There's nowhere to go."

Maureen glanced around the surrounding forest. Sara saw from the corner of her eye that the team had started to converge. Marco appeared beside her with his gun drawn. "I suggest you do as Sara says. Drop the bag, and no one gets hurt."

Maureen's eyes widened as she glanced down at her chest, which was lit up with tiny red dots like the lights on a Christmas tree. It wasn't until then that Maureen dropped the bag and eased down on her knees. The capture and arrest went off without incident, a little to Sara's dismay. She wanted to administer a little payback, maybe just a punch or two because Maureen had forced her to leave Collin and their newfound playtime.

Marco had her secured and in the back of his SUV as the agents converged on Collin's property and scoured the area for any sign of the stalker still at large. The search turned up empty, just like Sara thought it would. The stalker was using Maureen as a diversion, someone to keep Sara preoccupied and away from figuring out just who the hell she was, and that was something Sara was counting on.

"I'm ready to send my message."

# 17 CHAPTER

Marco leaned against the SUV and crossed his arms over his chest, clearly blocking the view of a sobbing Maureen in the backseat. "And what kind of message do you want to send?"

"It's time we put a name and a face to the stalker terrorizing Collin. It's time we draw her out and get her to come to us."

Sara explained her crazy-ass plan to Marco and, to her disbelief, Marco agreed to it. The plan was to stage Sara was hurt and to post it on Sanchez's blog and within the news media. She knew the stalker would come for her to finish the job, especially if she was deemed vulnerable. The news would report the apprehension of Maureen, along with the added bonus of reporting that Sara had a bullet wound to the arm and had been rushed to Regency General. It was time to draw out the stalker and end this game once and for all.

\*\*\*\*

Unable to relax, Collin was propped up against his headboard with the remote in his hand as he flipped through the television stations in search of something to pass the time and take his mind off his girlfriend. And she *was* his girlfriend. He just hadn't had the opportunity to tell her yet. A light knock came from his bedroom door.

He slid from the bed and pulled the door open, expecting to find his brother or one of the agents on the other side. What he hadn't expected to find was Regina with red, bloodshot, puffy eyes, crying at his threshold.

"What's wrong?" His first thoughts, knowing that Regina and Drew were in a relationship, was that something was wrong with Drew. When her silent cry turned into sobs, he did the first thing that came to mind. He pulled her into his chest and held her to calm the quivering woman that he'd come to rely on. It was an awkward moment and not very professional, but damn, he didn't know how else to handle a crying woman.

He glanced down at her. "Regina, you have to tell me what's wrong."

"What the hell did you do to her?" Drew bellowed from the other end of the hallway as he stomped toward Collin. He never seen his brother so pissed off. He glanced down at Regina and silently cursed.

Regina's eyes widened, and she gasped as Drew pushed between them and swung his fist, knocking Collin in the eye.

Collin staggered but held up his hands. "Man, I didn't do anything. She knocked on my door and was crying. I was just trying to get her to tell me what the problem was."

Drew looked as though he didn't believe it but still spun around and pulled Regina into his arms. "What's wrong, baby?" He lifted her chin with the crook of his finger. "Tell me why you're crying."

"It's all my fault." Regina pointed to the television, and they all turned. Collin reached for the remote and turned the volume up. A picture of Sara was posted in the corner.

Collin's legs gave out, and he dropped to sit on the end of the bed as he listened to the breaking report of how Carrington-Hill had captured Maureen but that Sara had been shot in the process and taken to Regency Memorial. His heart felt as though someone had it in a vise grip and was slowly squeezing the life out of him. He shook his head. *No, this is all wrong. This can't be happening. Not Sara.*

The report showed an image of an ambulance leaving the scene of what looked to be the house he'd grown up in. *What the hell is going on?* When the news switched to another story, he muted the television and turned back toward Regina. She was still shaking in Drew's arms.

"Drew, go get her some tea." Collin guided Regina to sit on his bed, and he got down on his knees in front of her. "Okay, start at the beginning and tell me everything that happened."

\*\*\*\*

Sara was propped in the reclining hospital bed, her arm in a makeshift sling with a gun hidden inside. Only a few more hours and the hospital halls would be empty. Marco had gone all out. He'd had the FBI commandeer the whole floor, not just a few of the rooms. More favors, she assumed he would have to pay back. Her father might have had a hand in staging the scene. Either way, it served her purpose. The room next to hers was set up as a monitoring room. A sign on the door indicated the room was under quarantine. Marco was a few doors down, in another room, set up to monitor the situation in case things turned bad.

The door to her room squeaked open, and Sara's mouth fell open. She snapped it shut as heat traveled up to her cheeks. The last person that needed to be anywhere near the stakeout had just walked in the door.

"Where's your detail?" Sara bellowed, sliding off the bed.

Collin moved to her side. "Ditched them with a little help from Drew. They were busy containing a fire that started in the woods. I had to come see you."

Sara squeezed her eyes closed as Collin cupped her cheek and kissed her forehead. "Are you in pain?" He motioned back toward the door with his thumb. "Do I need to go find a nurse?"

The comm in Sara's ear clicked to life. "You have incoming. Get him the hell out of there!"

Sara flicked the light off in the room and pushed Collin into the adjoining room. She whispered, "Stay here. No matter what you hear, you stay here until Marco comes to get you."

He shook his head, but she didn't have time to explain. She pulled the door closed and moved across the room to where the light switch was. Her dark clothes concealed her in shadows in the corner of the room. The comm clicked again. "Sara, I still can't tell who the hell she is. You're going to have to handle her blind. We're standing by for the signal. Just wait for her to make a move.

Sara stood in the corner, trying to slow down her breathing. She ditched the sling and held her gun pointed toward the ceiling. The ticking of the clock, in the room, gave away the minutes going by that would end this game once and for all. Here and now, it ended. No more chasing ghosts.

The door to the room squeaked open, letting in only a little light from the outside hallway, but still not giving Sara a good look at the stalker. The person lifted something in the air, and the next thing Sara saw was a bright white and red flash that accompanied the muffled sound of a gunshot. *A silencer.*

Sara aimed her weapon and flicked on the light. A moment's hesitation went through her as she registered the face with the name. Katrina, the sheriff's daughter, wearing a fake brown wig.

"Drop it, Katrina. The game's over."

Katrina went to lift the gun with the silencer at Sara, but never got off another shot. Sara aimed for Katrina's arm holding the gun and squeezed the trigger. The gun fell with a clank as Marco and the rest of the team converged on the room. Collin, who hadn't listened to her instructions, came in behind her and stopped cold in the middle of the room, starring at where a bleeding Katrina lay on the floor. Marco kicked the gun from her reach.

Katrina spotted Collin. "This is all your fault, Collin. It was supposed to be me. It was always supposed to be me. Tell them you don't love her. You love me."

Katrina turned her sneer toward Sara. "Why couldn't you just die, you bitch!"

Collin's mouth parted as he stood in the room, staring in shock. Nurses and a doctor helped Katrina to a gurney. Several of the team followed them out of the room with strict orders to never let her out of their sights.

Collin pulled Sara in his arms. "I'm so sorry." He pressed a kiss to her lips. "I swear I barely know her."

"It's not your fault." She cupped his cheek. She could see the relief in his eyes. She kissed him, not caring that Marco was a witness. "It's not your fault."

He took two steps away from her and held her gaze before he turned around and walked out of the hospital room. What the hell was he thinking? It's not like she could just leave and go after him, maybe knock some sense into him. She still had a job to do.

She had more to deal with than trying to console Collin. The FBI was already on site, but they'd also called the sheriff due to the circumstances, and she was going to be in debriefings and giving statements all night. They'd taken the gun and would find it matched the ballistics pulled from the murders and charge Katrina with those too.

# 18 CHAPTER

A knock sounded on his office door. "Collin, she's on line two again. Are you ready to talk to her?"

Collin glanced up from his keyboard. "No, and next time, Regina, I don't even want to know that she called."

Drew stepped into the room as Regina backed out of it. "Dude, you were a little harsh with Regina, don't you think?"

Collin tried ignoring his brother by clicking away at his keyboard, but Drew didn't go away. Abandoning his keyboard, Collin leaned back in his chair and let out a sigh, knowing that he would need to deal with Drew before he could get back to working. "Did you need something?"

Drew plopped down in one of the empty leather chairs and crossed an ankle over his knee. "No, but you do."

Collin raised his brow at the suggestion. No, he didn't need anything. Not anymore. "And what might that be?"

Drew rose from the chair and started pacing the length of the office. He waved his hands in the air. "I don't know. Maybe you need to see a shrink to help you get your head on straight or, hell, maybe just a good ass-kicking. Either one should work."

He stopped pacing and leaned against the chair. "You've been a jerk for the last few weeks, and now you're not even leaving the house. You've skipped all of your scheduled fundraisers and blown off appointments. You're like a lovesick schoolboy, and I'm starting to worry."

Collin huffed. "I haven't known her long enough to have fallen in love with her."

Drew shrugged. "Who gave you the impression there's an appropriate amount of time before you can fall in love? Honestly, dude, I thought you were smarter than that."

Collin rubbed his palm over his face, knowing his brother was right. "Drew, I almost got her killed. I can't take the chance that it will happen again."

Drew frowned. "No, *you* didn't almost get her killed. You aren't responsible for the psychos beyond your control. Her job is dangerous." He straightened and walked to the door before turning around. "We both know you miss her and want her to be a part of your life, no matter how much you deny it. I guess the real questions here are whether or not you can accept her career and if you'll still be able to win her back after you blew her off." Drew crossed his arms over his chest. "Because I hate to be the bearer of bad news, but you've screwed up big time." Drew shrugged. "You've blown her off for almost a month. She's a strong woman, but even the strongest have to draw a line somewhere." Drew patted the doorframe and disappeared down the hall.

Maybe his brother was right. He had some tough decisions in front of him, decisions that could potentially affect the rest of his life.

Regina walked in and dropped the mail on his desk without a word and turned to leave. She deserved a raise. He hadn't meant to snap at her every time Sara had called, but the mere mention of her name had him longing to be with her, be near her.

"Regina."

She turned around and raised her brow.

"I'm sorry I've been a grump for the last few weeks."

"More like an ass if you ask me."

Collin gave a slight nod of acknowledgement. "I am sorry."

Regina turned to leave but hesitated and turned back. "You know…she told me she won't be calling back and, if you ask me, I can't say that I blame her."

Regina spun on her heel and left Collin alone with nothing but his thoughts. Thoughts that included the little brunette that starred in his dreams.

\*\*\*\*

After everything calmed down, Sara tried to reach Collin to no avail. Regina politely told her that he was busy and that she'd tell him she'd called. First a week went by then three with no word from the man. She tried to resume a normal life by volunteering at the dog shelter to take her mind off Collin, but even that hadn't worked when she'd realized that her favorite pooch had finally been adopted. Realization hit her hard that she was truly all alone.

It was going to be tough for her to act happy at Lexi's wedding when Sara's own life was such a mess, but she'd prevail. She always did. Sara pushed all thoughts of Collin out of her mind and squared her shoulders before walking into the bridal suite to be pampered while she and her friends got ready for the wedding. There was no way she'd be the one responsible for ruining her best friend's big day. Nope, it wasn't going to happen, especially over a man.

Sara relaxed and sipped champagne while manicurists, makeup artists, and hairdressers reformed her from the tomboy she was to the princess her mother always wanted her to be.

Sara's thoughts returned to a comment that Lexi had made the first time she'd laid eyes on Collin. He was supposed to be her date but here she sat, dateless. Not even an offer from Garrett had cheered her up. Her heart ached; she'd been unable to sleep or eat and, by the looks of the extra room in her dress, she might have even lost some weight. Not that losing weight was ever a bad thing, but she'd never experienced it because of a guy. Not until now. She must have had that poor-pitiful-me look on her face because Lexi interrupted her thoughts.

"He hasn't even called you back yet?"

"I gave up about a week ago." She sipped her champagne, hoping the alcohol would drown away the memories. It didn't.

Catherine reached over and patted her hand. "Maybe he's just been busy or needs time to come to terms with everything that's happened."

She shook her head. "Let's just face it, ladies, it was over before it started." She rose, and tightened the sash of her robe. "Besides, relationships that start under extreme duress hardly ever work out." She glanced at Lexi and smiled feeling truly happy for her best friend. "Except yours, Lexi." Thinking of Catherine's similar experience she turned toward her other best friend. "And yours."

She plopped back down in her chair when the realization hit her that it wasn't the circumstances; it was the men. Lexi and Catherine's boyfriends had realized they couldn't live without them. What did that say about Collin and his feelings or lack of feelings for her? She lowered her head. "What were the odds that lightning would strike a third time?"

Lexi and Catherine moved to her side. "If he hasn't come to his senses by now, then he doesn't deserve you."

A knock sounded on the door before an older lady popped her head in to announce. "Ladies, five minutes ladies."

She was saved from more of the clichés she'd heard all of her life. They pulled on their dresses, helped Lexi with her veil, grabbed their flowers and walked out into the hall, moving into position like a well-choreographed maneuver. Sara chuckled as she wondered whether Trip realized that even though he was marrying Lexi, he was not only getting a wife, but the added bonus of having the new wife's best friends around also; her gun carrying best friends. Sara smiled. *Three peas in a pod.*

The wedding was quick, but the reception lasted all night. Lights twinkled around the room and the flowers were to die for. The food was scrumptious and the crowd was having fun dancing to the band. Lexi smiled at her husband before sharing a kiss, and stolen glances between the two, lifted Sara's heart. That was exactly the kind of love she wanted for herself.

Sara's gaze landed on Catherine. She was giggling on the dance floor as she tried to help her fiancé conquer the moves to the line dance.

People young and old enjoyed themselves, some sitting around the tables talking, others with drinks in their hand and, like Catherine, even more were on the dance floor trying to do a line dance that Sara had never heard of. She'd been asked to dance several times by Garrett and others she worked with, along with a few of the groom's friends. She'd let herself escape from reality and actually enjoyed herself for the rest of the evening.

She'd successfully pushed all thoughts of Collin to the back of her mind, and it had worked. She'd laughed and danced and enjoyed the joyous occasion and determined that life wouldn't end because of Collin Martin. She'd been fine before he came into her life, and she'd be fine after. Especially after the trip to the beach house she had scheduled.

****

Sara arrived at her most favorite place in the world. She had her bikini on beneath her clothes and dragged her suitcase up the porch steps and into the beach house. It had been months since the last time she'd been here and almost six years since the last time she'd been to the beach house alone, without Lexi and Catherine joining her for their yearly excursions. The caretakers had mentioned that the place was stocked and ready for company when she'd called to inquire and warn them that she'd be having more people than usual on this trip. Husbands and boyfriends would be showing up also. Even though Sara didn't have a significant other, her friends wouldn't make her feel like a fifth wheel.

She ditched the suitcase in the living room, grabbed a towel and bottled water, and walked out the French doors overlooking the ocean. The familiar smell of the salt water drifted to her nose as she lifted her face to the sun. She inhaled a deep breath as she threw the towel over her shoulder and took the steps down to the sand two at a time. This was her favorite place to swim. Lexi found her release in jogging for miles on end, Catherine enjoyed laying out in the sun, but Sara found hers in swimming. She discarded her towel and clothes and walked through the rolling waves and into the caressing water of the ocean.

She submerged in the water and swam half a mile off shore before she returned. After making her way back up to the beach, she wiped the salt from her face and was toweling off when she heard a dog barking up toward her house.

She recognized the barking as Spike's immediately and dropped to her knees to prepare for impact. He launched himself at her, and she caught him in the air, causing her to land on her back. Spike's long pink tongue attacked her next. His wet doggy kisses covered her face as she rubbed his ears and laughed.

**\*\*\*\***

Collin rounded the house in search of the mangy mutt that had jumped out of the car and took off. The dog was starting to grow on him. That was when he spotted Sara on the beach. Collin couldn't take his eyes off her. Her smile was like a sunrise after a rainstorm. It brightened everything and everyone around her, like a fresh scent the morning after a hard rain, clearing the air and making everything new and more alive. His heart ached at the thought that he'd almost given up hope on their relationship. He had almost let her walk out of his life.

She rubbed Spike's ears and asked. "Who brought you here baby? Was it Lexi or Catherine?"

Collin moved to the steps and sat down, watching and waiting, unable to predict her mood. Her smile slowly started to fall when she noticed him sitting on her steps. The happiness he'd witnessed moments ago vanished from her face. She stood and brushed the sand from her legs before grabbing her towel.

She marched toward the stairs with Spike on her heels. She bypassed him and galloped up the steps.

"What are you doing here?" she asked without even glancing over her shoulder. She was pissed all right, and he couldn't blame her.

"I missed you."

She threw her head back and laughed as he followed her into the house. She moved to the kitchen, grabbed a bowl, filled it with water, and set it on the floor for Spike. Well, at least one of them was getting a decent greeting. He envied the mangy mutt, wishing she was stroking him instead of the dog.

"You're about a month too late, Mr. Martin," she said before taking a sip of her water.

He wiggled a finger as he stepped closer to her. "I'm afraid we have unfinished business to discuss."

She swallowed the water and squeezed the plastic bottle. "No, I don't think we do. I caught your stalker, exposed your business manager, and kept you alive. I finished our business."

He stepped within arm's reach but didn't breach the barrier. "You were supposed to make me dateable, and I'm afraid you've ruined me for all other women."

She stepped toward him and poked him in the chest. "I can't claim credit for that, Mr. Martin." She poked him again only this time harder. "I can't change what doesn't want to be changed." She lowered her hand. "And, to be honest, I'm not sure I want to continue to try."

Collin took her hand in his and kissed the finger she'd just used to put him in his place. "Forgive me, Sara. I was a fool, and I'm miserable without you." Spike trotted over to her side and barked. "We both miss you."

Sara shook her head and dropped her gaze, as if unable to look him in the eye. This was the first time he'd ever seen this vulnerable side of her. She was cautious, and it broke his heart that he was responsible.

He lifted her chin with the crook of his finger. "Sara, I'm falling in love with you. Please just give us a chance."

Her gaze searched his face, searching for what he didn't know, but he damn sure hoped she found it. She frowned. "Collin, you don't love me." She gestured between both of them. "What we had was an illusion. It wasn't real."

He pulled her into his arms and pressed his lips against hers, kissing her with the same ferocity they'd shared that night in his room, with the same desire and passion only she brought out in him. Only when she sagged in his arms did he pull away. "Tell me that wasn't real, Sara. Tell me you don't still want me as much as I want you. That you don't lie awake every night thinking about me like I do you."

A tear trickled down her cheek, and he swiped it away with the pad of his thumb. "Our lives are too different."

"I like my life so much more with you in it. Please, Sara, just say you'll try."

He'd left himself wide open, bared his heart and his soul and handed it to her on a silver platter. It seemed like an eternity ticked by but it was probably more like mere seconds before she broke the silence that stretched between them.

"On one condition, Collin."

He couldn't help the grin that spread across his lips. He pulled her into his arms with relief. "Name it, and it's yours."

"If for some reason things don't work out...I want shared custody of Spike."

Collin chuckled as relief filled every fiber of his body. "Deal."

# 19 CHAPTER

*One Year Later*

Sara settled against Collin's broad chest and into the comfort of her lover's arms as she watched the dancing red embers in the fireplace and listened to the crackle and pop of the wood, the only sounds breaching the serenity of the beach house. The serenity would be short-lived because, by morning, the beach house might seem a bit overcrowded when Lexi, Catherine, and their significant others started showing up. She stroked the dog's fine black hairs as he snuggled against her legs. Never would she have thought for a second, even in her crazy life that she'd have such inner peace. Yes, she still chased the bad guys and cheating husbands, but

217

every night, she now had Collin to come home to, and that changed everything.

Spike jumped down and settled on to the rug sitting in front of the fire place.

Glancing up at Collin, she smiled. "Thank you."

He leaned down and kissed her cheek. "For what, baby?"

She turned in his arms, straddled his lap, and pressed a tender kiss to Collin's lips. "For being the man I never knew I needed."

The lines on his face softened. "I can't imagine my life without you in it, Sara. I hope one day you'll make an honest man out of me and finally accept my proposal."

Sara smiled as her heart swelled. "I love you, Collin Martin, and sometime very soon I'll be the person responsible for removing you from the bachelor list. You can count on it."

Spike barked three times in a row, even though he didn't move from his nest by the fire.

Collin laughed. "He seems to like that idea. Why don't we make him happy and set a date?"

She leaned in closer and kissed his neck. "Is tomorrow too soon?"

He cupped her butt, rose, and started walking back to the room. "I think I can keep you so worn out that, between now and then, you won't change your mind."

Collin kicked the door closed behind them and did just what he promised and the next day on the beach with her two best friends as her witnesses... so did she.

Thank you for taking the time to read my stories. As always I appreciate each and every one of you. If you liked it and have a moment, please leave a review on Amazon.

## ABOUT THE AUTHOR

Kate has lived in Florida for most of her entire life. She enjoys a quiet life with her husband, Michael and two kids.

Kate has pulled all-nighters finishing her favorite books and also writing them. She says she'll sleep when she's dead or when her muse stops singing off key.

She loves creating worlds full of suspense, secrets, hunky men, kick ass heroines, steamy sex and oh yeah the love of a lifetime. Not to mention an occasional ghost and other supernatural talents thrown into the mix.

23745265R00144

Made in the USA
Middletown, DE
02 September 2015